TWO SONS OF SATAN

When Buck McKee and his partner Tortilla Joe arrive at Buckskin, Arizona, they find Jack Perry — son of Sam Perry, for whom they punched cows in Texas — has been framed for murder and lynched at the instigation of Curt Lawrence, who is plotting to rule the land. Dramatic and desperate action follows when these Two Sons of Satan take a hand.

Books by Brett Austin
in the Linford Western Library:

GAMBLERS GUN LUCK
ARIZONA SADDLES

BRETT AUSTIN

◆

TWO SONS OF SATAN

Complete and Unabridged

LINFORD
Leicester

First published in Great Britain

First Linford Edition
published May 1994

British Library CIP Data

Austin, Brett
    Two sons of Satan.—Large print ed.—
Linford western library
I. Title II. Series
813.52 [F]

ISBN 0–7089–7572–0

Published by
F. A. Thorpe (Publishing) Ltd.
Anstey, Leicestershire
Set by Words & Graphics Ltd.
Anstey, Leicestershire
Printed and bound in Great Britain by
T. J. Press (Padstow) Ltd., Padstow, Cornwall

This book is printed on acid-free paper

1

Desert Death

THE wind howled across the Arizona desert. It bent *mesquite* and sagebrush, and it made an eerie sound as it whistled through desert willows. Even ghost trees had to bow before the demands of the hard wind. Head bowed, Buck McKee, the tall Texan, rode into the wind, with his partner, Tortilla Joe, the Mexican, taking the lead. Their weary horses plodded forward, hoofs shuffling on sand.

They were rounding the toe of a small hummock when suddenly a rider roared out of nowhere. He rode in wild haste and, because of the thick sandstorm, he did not see Tortilla Joe's horse until the two broncs had collided. The rider's horse hit that of

1

the fat Mexican head-on.

"What een heck ees thees — ?"

Tortilla Joe's startled yelp jerked up Buck McKee's head. Hurriedly the lanky Texan reined his horse to one side, thereby escaping the kicking entanglement of horseflesh.

Because the wind had been blowing the wrong direction neither partner had heard the rider approach. Tortilla Joe's horse lay on its right side, kicking like a wounded jackrabbit. The fat Mexican sat on the sand, his thick jowls showing a wild, startled look.

Buck McKee looked at the other rider, and surprise touched his high-cheekboned, sun-tanned face. This rider also sat on the sand, about ten feet away from where Tortilla Joe sat. The rider's mount — a sweat-streaked sorrel gelding — had painfully staggered to its feet. Now it stood with its off-foreleg lifted, plainly in pain. But Buck was not interested in the lamed saddler. He had all his interest focused on the strange rider.

2

For the rider was not a man. The rider was a young woman — and a lovely one, at that. Her hat, hanging by the jaw-strap, lay on her back, exposing a mass of black, shiny hair. Her face was small and, right now, it showed anger.

Buck saw a rather thin face, and the mouth seemed rather severe for one that young, but he blamed this on the duress of the moment. She tugged at her buckskin riding skirt, for it had slipped above her knees. She had very nice looking knees, Buckshot McKee noticed instantly.

"Quit gawking at my knees, you long-eared baboon!"

Buck grinned. She had a temper, too. Quickly he went out of saddle. Three strides of his long legs, and he was beside her. He winked at Tortilla Joe, still sitting on the sand, and the girl did not see the wink.

"Did you skin your knee, Miss?"

She tugged at her riding skirt and hid her knees. "Keep your hands off my person!" she warned. Again, she jerked at her dress. "And I can get up alone, too! If you two galoots had only watched where you were going — Oh, my ankle!"

Buck had her by both elbows. He was still grinning like a monkey who had just discovered an open paint can.

"Maybe it's busted," he said.

"You sound — hopeful," she said hurriedly. "I got to take the trail again — They're chasing me — "

"But you just got here," Buck joked. "We like your company, don't we, Tortilla Joe?"

The Mexican nodded. "We sure does, Mees — "

She did not give her name, though. She hobbled a little, getting her ankle in shape to hold her weight. Buck stood, hands on hips, and watched, a satanic grin on his wide mouth.

"You sprained your nigh leg. Your bronc has sprained his off leg. You two should have worked together and sprained legs on the same side. And by

4

the way, Miss — who is chasin' you, and why?"

"Oh, close your big mouth!"

Buck smiled wider. Tortilla Joe grinned, but he remained sitting. He seemed to be so lazy he did not want to get to his feet.

Buck said, "A frosty little girl, eh? Tortilla, you down for the day — or do you figure to walk again?"

Laboriously the fat Mexican got to his feet. He seemed to be all right; shock had passed, and his dark face was smiling. The girl almost fell, and again Buck McKee got her by both elbows.

"Get your hands — off me — "

Buck said, "I'll give the matter proper thought. You got a nice set of elbows, Miss. They're soft and feel good, and they sure are tanned and well-formed — Ouch!"

She swung a right hand, intending to slap him. Buck ducked hurriedly and stepped back and she almost fell. Buck kept on grinning and she spat at him. Then she hobbled over to a

5

granite boulder. She had tears in her eyes. Buck wondered whether they were caused by pain or by anger.

He decided to stop teasing her. Her ankle might even be broken. Anyway, it was sprained — and sometimes a sprain was as bad as a break, if not worse. Buck therefore said nothing.

Tortilla Joe looked at his horse which, by this time, had struggled to its feet. The bronc had all four hoofs on the ground and stood in apparently good shape.

"My *caballo*, he ees all right, Buckshot," the Latin said. He panted his words. "But the weend — she ees steel knocked out from under my ribs." Suddenly he cocked his dark, heavy head and he seemed to be listening to something which Buck had not yet heard.

"What do you hear, Tortilla Joe?"

The Mexican wet his thick bottom lip. "First, I hears the weend — all the time, the weend. Then, I hears something else, Buckshots."

6

"What is it?"

"Somewhere I hear riders an' they come thees way — and they come at a fast pace — You hear them now, no?"

"I hear them," Buck said.

Suddenly, pain left the girl's face. She was on her feet, her limp completely gone now.

"Riders coming?" she demanded.

"I hear them," Buck said. "Sounds like quite a bunch of them. This sandstorm — hides them — Hey, where you going, young lady?"

"I got to get away from them!" The young girl panted her words. "If they catch me — I got to get to Cinchring camp. I got to get help for Jack — They'll lynch him, unless I get help!"

Buck stared at her. The hoofs of the horses came closer — they rode at a hard pace, breasting the sandstorm. Tortilla Joe stared, tongue idle on his bottom lip.

"Who they lynch named Jack?" the Mexican asked.

"You two don't know him — you're strangers here. I know every man on this range — you two don't fit in . . . But I'll tell you — and then I got to get out fast — They aim to lynch Jack Perry!"

Buck said, "Jack Perry . . . Now who aims to hang Perry — and for what reason, woman — ?"

But he got no answer. Unexpectedly she darted toward Buck's horse. Despite her lame ankle, she moved like a frightened antelope. Tortilla Joe, guessing at her idea, tried to grab her. He might just as well have grabbed for a hunk of the wind. Buck caught his partner by a wide shoulder.

"Let her go, Tortilla!"

"Buck, she ees goin' to steal your horse, no!"

"Let her go!"

She was already in the saddle. The stirrups, stretched out to fit Buck's long legs, were too long for her — therefore she put her feet in the leathers, using these for stirrups. Her quirt rose and

8

fell and the startled horse roared away, with her words whipping back over her shoulder.

"Thanks for the use — of your bronc! I'll bring him back — when I get done with him — "

Then, she was gone around a sand hummock. And Buck McKee looked thoughtfully at solemn Tortilla Joe, who in turn gazed back at his partner.

"Always," the Mexican said slowly, "there ees the troubles for us, Buckshots. When weel our troubles they weel end?"

"When we're both dead, I reckon. Did she say *Jack Perry*?"

"That name she deed say, Buckshots. And what ees the more, she ees say somebody he ees aimin' to lynch our *amigo*, Jack Perry?"

"That's what she said, Tortilla Joe."

Tortilla Joe shook his heavy head. "I wonder who the girl she was, and why they chase her? And why they want to lynch our friend, and for where is the lynchin' to take place?"

Buck shrugged.

The hoofs roared closer. Both of the partners turned. Now they could see the riders. They spilled over a hill and they rode with hard and patent purpose. They were a colourful outfit.

Gaudy pintos — black and bay and grey — were in the group. One man rode a long-legged bay; another sat saddle on a deep sorrel. They saw the partners and came towards them, dust kicking under steel shod hoofs. They swerved to evade catclaw and sagebrush, and they roared across the bottom of the dry wash toward the partners.

Buck and Tortilla Joe watched. Tortilla Joe's thick face held an almost stupid look, but Buck knew back of that apparent docility was an alert awareness. This Mexican could show a very deceptive face. As for himself, Buck felt danger tug at his innards, building a cold wall around his belly. These men were not out looking for cattle or running wild horses.

They rode with swift intent, and they were after the girl, Buck realized. Danger was in the wind.

Buck turned and looked toward the direction taken by the fleeing woman. She was out of sight. The wind, he realized, had died down somewhat; its wild fury had blown itself out, and now it was tapering off. But he had no thought for the wind. Jack Perry, according to the strange woman, was in danger of losing his life.

Buck put his thoughts into words. "Judging from past experiences, they lynch men because those men have killed somebody. This girl said they aimed to lynch Jack Perry. Therefore he must have killed somebody."

"And thees girl — she ees ride to Ceenchring Camp, wherever or whatever eet ees — Hola, that man in the lead — he ees a big fellow, Buckshots."

"Plenty of man there," Buck had to admit.

2

Rough Range

THEY came in fast, reining their blowing broncs. And the big man was in the lead. He was big in body, and arrogance had marked him. He rode a tough black-and-grey pinto, sitting a hand-engraved Phoenix saddle. He wore a wide Stetson hat and the chin-straps, meeting under his craggy jaw, were held together by a shiny gold nugget that now glistened in the sun.

Buck saw that a buckskin-jacket, gaudy with red and black beads, covered his wide shoulders and thick chest. He saw a flaming red shirt and the man wore new California pants under wide-winged Cheyenne chaps.

Behind him, were his riders. Buck gave them all a momentary glance.

They packed Winchester rifles in saddle-scabbards and each carried a shortgun, and one or two even toted two pistols. Guns were tied-down and Buck thought, this is a tough outfit, and he looked back at the big young leader.

The man's eyes, glistening and steely, ran over to the lamed sorrel. When he spoke his voice had a superior edge that somehow rubbed against Buck McKee's good nature.

"Where's the girl?" he demanded.

Buck grinned. "She done got away," he said slowly. "She done stole my bronc an' *boom* — afore I could hold her, she was gone!"

"She stole your horse, you say?"

Buck nodded. "You heard me rightly, Mister Man. She lights into my saddle, and here I am — with her crippled sorrel." He assumed a hangdog appearance. "Ain't no justice in this here world — "

The young man stood on stirrups, looking in the direction taken by the young woman. The storm had blown itself out and the horizon was rapidly clearing.

His face took on a hard look. "Yonder she rides, men! Over there, and she's so far away a man could never catch her. Our broncs are winded and the chase is over. Thanks to these two strangers, she got away."

They turned hostile eyes on Buck and Tortilla Joe. Probing eyes that held anger and rough emotion. The blame for letting this girl escape was laid on the shoulders of the partners.

The big leader said sternly, "Forget the heifer, men." Wind blew hard against him suddenly, then spent its fury. His pale blue eyes rested on Buckshot McKee and Tortilla Joe.

"Who are you two strange buckos?" His voice held authority. "And what for you riding this Salt River country over here in Arizona Territory?"

His voice was harsh and rough as desert sand. It was the voice of a man accustomed to giving orders . . . and having those orders quickly obeyed. It rubbed against Buckshot like sandpaper. And when the lanky cowpuncher spoke his own voice held naked authority.

"I could ask you the same questions, fellow!"

Behind the big leader a man stirred in leather, hand going toward his holstered gun. Buck flipped him a quick glance and the man stared at him with dull eyes. Buck looked back at the leader.

A merciless grin, tough and narrow, touched the thin lips, giving the eyes a slanting rough look. A big hand went up and played with the gold nugget that held the chin-straps together under the big jaw. Big knuckles moved, long fingers shoved the nugget up and down the straps. Behind him a horse rolled the cricket in his bit, the sound suddenly shrill and potent with danger.

The big leader spoke slowly. "I take it you two buttons are newcomers to this Hammerhead range. Am I correct on this assumption?"

15

Buck nodded. Tortilla Joe's heavy head bobbed up and down. The Mexican said nothing; he was leaving all conversation to his partner, a habit of his in time of trouble and stress.

"You're on Hammerhead range."

Buck studied him. "Hammerhead range, eh? Well, it means nothing to me, fellow. Me an' my partner was ridin' along in the sandstorm when this woman rides plumb into my partner's bronc. Both horses go down. The wind muffled her coming. She's got nice knees, fellows."

A rider laughed.

The big man turned on stirrups. He sent a hard glance towards the man who was laughing. The man closed his mouth and became glum. Then the big man returned his gaze to Tortilla Joe and Buckshot McKee.

Buck had a moment of raw anxiety. The girl had said they were going to lynch Jack Perry. And Jack was the son of an old, old friend of theirs, cowman Sam Perry.

16

"She'll never git to Cinchring camp in time to get help into Buckskin town," a man said slowly. "By the time them Perry construction hands git into Buckskin, Jack Perry will be hangin' high an' dead, Curt."

The big man nodded. He seemed to suddenly become agreeable and friendly. "My name is Curt Lawrence," he told Buck and the Mexican. He emphasized the word *Lawrence*. Buck got the impression that the name was supposed to mean something on this desert range. "Now who are you two drifters?"

Buck gave the riders his name and introduced Tortilla Joe. "This gal mentioned something about this gent named Jack Perry," he said. "Why for do they aim to lynch the fellow?"

"He killed my dad, old John Lawrence." Suddenly Curt Lawrence's brows drew down and gave him a predatory look. "Say, your names sound familiar, men."

Buck asked, "How come?"

"Do you two know Jack Perry?"

Buck played ignorant. He was learning nothing darned fast. "Never heard of Jack Perry until now," he assured.

Curt Lawrence said slowly, "Seems to me I've heard your handles mentioned before now . . . Seems to me Jack Perry boasted about a couple of drifters coming into this area to side him. And, unless my memory proves wrong — which it seldom does — them two gunmen were to tote the names you just mentioned to me, McKee . . . "

A stiffness had gone through the riders. Buck could feel it and taste it and sense it. Hard eyes were on him and Tortilla Joe. Eyes that appraised and watched with wary steeliness.

Curt Lawrence toted a pearl-handled six-shooter. Now his right hand, big and thick-knuckled, rested on the gun's grip. The air was knife-sharp with suspicion and controlled violence.

Buck glanced at Tortilla Joe.

The Mexican's tongue, as wide as that of an ox, came out slowly and

18

attempted to dampen thick lips. Dark, short fingers rested on the handle of the old .45 in its well-oiled holster.

And the Mexican's eyes, seemingly dark and seemingly child-innocent, moved from one man to another, touching this man, and that man. They took silent stock of this tough danger.

Buck saw that this situation called for caution and the correct words. The main thing was to get to Buckskin town and keep the citizens from hanging Jack Perry. The thought came that lynching would not take place until the old wolf's son, Curt Lawrence, could officiate, for Jack Perry had killed Curt's father, and what would be more fitting than to have the son kick out the trap?

Buck and Tortilla Joe had never seen Jack Perry. But he was old Sam Perry's only offspring and they were deep in debt to old Sam, who ran a cow-spread up in Colorado.

Again Curt Lawrence spoke. "How

about it, you two? You two gunhands comin' in to side Jack Perry?"

Buck shook his head. "Never heard of the name before," he lied.

Curt Lawrence nodded, eyes scheming. "Okay . . . " he said, but Buck knew the matter was not ended.

Buck said, "We need grub. We need shaves and haircuts. We need some sleep on a good bed, not the ground. My partner's bronc is broke to tote double. Why not all of us head into Buckskin town, after we unsaddle the girl's bronc." He looked at Curt Lawrence. "What handle does that prairie-chicken travel under, Lawrence?"

"Her name is Clair McCullen. She'll bring your horse back, McKee. Get on behind the Mexican and ride back with us, and move pronto."

Buck stood stock-still. He studied the big man with cold insolence. "Are you trying to order me around, Lawrence?"

Again, that stiffness, binding these men in a unit, freezing them tight in

20

saddles. Evidently nobody ever spoke roughly to this son of the dead cattle-king. But Lawrence smiled, although the smile was forced.

"You're a salty rooster, McKee . . . Somebody might pull your tail-feathers, fellow, if you stick around Salt River long enough . . ."

"It won't be you," Buck warned.

Tortilla Joe said, "Forgets it, you two," and he swung into saddle. He left his left stirrup free and Buck put his boot into it. Buck lifted his length across the horse and settled behind the cantle. Tortilla Joe restored his boot to the stirrup.

"Come on, men," Lawrence ordered.

The posse swung its horses and rode back in the direction from whence it had come. Buck bounced a little, arms around Tortilla Joe. They loped across the sand wash, horses kicking sand and gravel. They almost ran over a jackrabbit, which suddenly leaped out from under a sagebrush.

The darting rabbit, jumping out of

21

the sagebrush, made Curt Lawrence's bronc shy, and the big man, anger grooving his face, hit his bronc solidly with his quirt, straightening him out. For a moment, then, Buck saw raw, terrible violence on the big face, and he knew that the man was driven by harsh passions. And, because he knew this, he knew that Curt Lawrence, when aroused, was dangerous.

"Bone headed bronc," the big man snarled. "Three gaits, the fool — walk, stumble, and fall down. Make good glue, he would!"

"Too tough for glue," a rider hollered. "The Hammerhead is a tough spread, and its broncs are too tough for the glue factory, Curt!"

Buck did some thinking. He added up a few facts and he got some answers. This thing was clear to him now, he figured. He and Tortilla Joe had been heading for Yuma, the town down on the Colorado river on the corner of Arizona Territory and the State of California. They were heading that direction to get a job punching cows for Gallatin, who ran a spread right at the junction of the Gila and Colorado Rivers. Fall of the year had taken possession of the Colorado country, where they had spent the summer punching cows for old Sam Perry. Soon there would be snow, and both hated snow.

So they had asked old Sam Perry for their time. Faded blue eyes had studied them under heavy eyebrows.

"So you two aim to drift out, eh?" the old cowman had asked.

Both of the partners thought the world of old Sam. Sam had bailed them out of jail that spring, for the partners had got into a little trouble. The trouble had consisted of starting a gangfight and breaking the windows and furniture to smithereens in a local saloon. Sam had got them out of jail by using his influence with the judge and sheriff. Had it not been for old Sam, the partners would still have been in jail, up there in Colorado.

Buck had nodded. "Drifting south, Sam. Thanks for the boost and the summer wages. Up here a man spends all his summer wages buying winter clothes. Know an old bird named Gallatin — down in south-west Arizona — and he's got a winter job for us. Don't need to buy no winter clothes down under that hot sun."

"Lucky dogs. Can drift when you want to. Not tied down to anything . . . " Old Sam had counted out gold pieces. Arthritis had made his once supple fingers into talons. "Do me a favour, men?"

"Name it," Buck had said.

"When you cross the Continental Devide, you come down into the Salt River desert. Swing south into a little town called Buckskin an' give my greetings to my only boy, Jack."

Buck had been startled. "Never knowed you had a boy, Sam. Never heard you mention him."

The old man's eyes had become dreamy. "Never have seen Jack for eight long years, men. But he's a busy one, that boy of mine. Right now he's developin' some desert land down there — irrigation, I figure. Yep, eight long years — whale of a long time for a man not to see his only offspring."

Buck had promised, "Be glad to give him your greetings, Sam."

"The cook is goin' write Jack a letter today — write it for me. With this rheumatiz, I cain't write good no longer. Never was no hand with a pen, either. I'll warn him you two is comin'. Stay out of bar-room fights and jails, men. And don't forgit your old friend, Sam Perry."

They had shaken hands. "We'll be back next summer," Buck had promised.

Tortilla Joe had said, "We punch cows gain next sommer for our old *amigo*. You can bet the life on that, Samuel."

Evidently the cook had written the letter. Evidently the letter had reached Buckskin ahead of them, which was

25

C-1

natural. They had loafed along, angling down toward the Gallatin spread. No hurry. Taking their time, riding along, enjoying God and Nature. Evidently the cook had mentioned to Jack Perry that two friends of the old gent, named Tortilla Joe and Buck McKee, would drop in. And somehow Curt Lawrence had gotten hold of this information. But the names had not registered with enough impact, and Lawrence was doubtful. But the impact would come later, Buck thought with a wry smile.

Curt Lawrence saw that smile. "Something funny, McKee?" he murmured.

Buck said, "Smiled at your ugly face, Lawrence."

Evidently the cowman had a hidden sense of humour, for apparently Buck's words did not rankle him, or maybe he did not get angry because of Buck's wide grin.

"You're a rough gent, McKee. You blundered into trouble right off the bat. I take it you two are getting this shave and haircut, fillin' your bellies full of restaurant chuck, and then you're drifting on, I figure."

"An order?" Buck asked.

Now the man was hard. The humour was gone, his face was bleak, his words were chopped.

"Judge for yourself, McKee."

Buck felt the push of impatience. They had to reach Buckskin and keep old Sam Perry's only son from being hanged —

"I'm a bettin' man," Buck told Lawrence.

Lawrence studied him. "You want to bet I cain't run you off Hammerhead range?"

Buck grinned and shook his head. "They's two of us astraddle this old nag. Only one man on your pinto. But a pinto hoss, I still say, ain't got no bottom." He sent a scornful glance over the other mounts. "Hammerhead outfits rides pore horseflesh, looks to me. I'm still a bettin' man, Lawrence."

"Which way does your bets run?"

"Even with a double load, this Mexican's bronc can outrun that mangy pinto — and leave the other Hammerhead hosses behind, too!"

A number of men laughed. Curt Lawrence showed a smug grin. "We runs good horseflesh on Hammerhead, McKee. Your eyes has been affected by the wind and desert heat. By the way, have you got a few bucks under your belt that you'd feel like usin' to tempt fickle Fate?"

Buck nodded. "Twenty bucks, in gold. Coin of the realm, Curt Lawrence. Bite into it and it bites good . . . "

Lawrence scoffed, "Chicken feed, fella. But, a deal — if it's all you got. Okay, scissorbills, let's hit the gravel wide open. Try to keep from eatin' the big rocks, McKee!"

They roared towards Buckskin. Tortilla Joe rode like a jockey, gross body leaning forward, shoulders bent to deflect the wind. He knew how to get every ounce of energy out of his horse. Buck hung on to the Mexican,

28

also bending forward, and occasionally he glanced back at Curt Lawrence, who whipped his horse with savage slashes of his shot-loaded quirt.

The sun was hot, slipping down behind high igneous peaks. Dust rose and the wind whistled around granite boulders. A catclaw branch hit Buck, catching his shirt sleeve, the spines reaching through the shirt and tearing his forearm. It hurt. But he had no time to nurse his wounds now.

Hammerhead broncs had been ridden hard in pursuit of Clair McCullen. Buck and Tortilla Joe had loafed along; therefore the Mexican's horse was fresh while Hammerhead horseflesh was winded. Buck had not expected that the horse, carrying two riders, could have outrun the Hammerhead horses; such, though, was proving the case.

He had merely wanted to get more speed up to get into Buckskin sooner. As it was, despite its double load, Tortilla Joe's mount forged ahead. They raced across another sand wash, then hit a wagon road that angled through sagebrush.

"Take the road," Buck shouted in his partner's dark ear.

"We beat them, Buckshot!"

"Thet little signboard back there said it was still a mile into Buckskin," Buckshot McKee warned. "By that time this old hay-burner might be fagged out, totin' both of us."

"He good horse."

"Get your big carcass down so you don't stop so much wind."

Grinning widely, the Latin crouched down, lying along the mane of his horse. Buck also bent his body forward. Now the Hammerhead men were swinging their broncs on to the wagon-road.

They were inching up when the partners rode into Buckskin. The town was a weather-beaten and sun-burned little burg sitting on small mesa, and surrounded by sandhills and sagebrush. Mesquite grew in clumps and juniper trees and scrub oak dotted the hills, green clumps jumping out of the brown bareness. Saguaro cacti rose and held up their spiny arms. Some of the saguaros were very old and very big, reaching around forty feet in height.

But Buck had no eyes for the cacti.

From out of an alley came a cur, fangs snapping. Gaunt, shaggy, he snarled in, leaping for the hamstrings of Tortilla Joe's bronc. But the horse was no newcomer and he leaped, almost throwing Buck who hung on, the saddlestrings cutting his hands.

Buck glanced back.

The dog, missing his lunge, had rolled over. Now Hammerhead broncs, roaring in, rode him down. One kicked him and he rolled end over end. Buck saw him get to his feet, yelp, and dart back into the alley.

Up ahead was a crowd, Buck saw.

And a motley crowd it was — grown-ups and children and dogs and even a burro. He saw the gay flash of a Mexican *serape*, the wide-brimmed sombrero of a Mexican *vaguero*. Most of the kids, a glance told him, were Mexican children, and lots of them were rather unwashed.

They were grouped in front of a long adobe building. Squat and rambling, it hugged the hot earth, occupying almost a block.

But it was not the crowd — or the building — that claimed Buck's attention.

Tortilla Joe had drawn rein, and the sides of his horse moved in and out, as the bronc grabbed for air.

Tortilla Joe's eyes were wide, the pupils distended. Automatically his brown, dirty hand rose.

He made the Sign of the Cross.

Now the Hammerhead broncs, also blowing hard, were around Buck and Tortilla Joe. Curt Lawrence's pinto sobbed for breath. The young cowman leaned forward, stirrups holding his weight.

"You win, McKee."

Buck nodded.

Buck felt sick.

Curt Lawrence dug in his pocket and came out with a twenty-buck gold piece. He held it out to Buck.

"Here you are, McKee."

Curt Lawrence watched Buck. Buck made no move to reach for the coin.

Anger coloured Lawrence's face, for Buck paid him no attention. Buck's attention was riveted on the adobe building. Built in the proper Spanish style of architecture, it had jutting ceiling-joists.

Now, from one of these joists, hung the body of a man. And the wind moved in and turned the body and showed his hands bound behind him. His shadow danced on dust; his body hung limply; the rope had broken his neck.

"They beat us to it," a man murmured.

"Perry'll never murder another man," a man said hoarsely.

Buck thought, in that instance, of Old Sam Perry, up in Colorado. Back in the alley a hound lifted his nose and howled towards the blue bowl of the Arizona sky.

Buck shivered.

Curt Lawrence seemingly had no interest in the hanged man. "Here's your money, McKee," he repeated.

Buck slapped the gold piece to the ground.

Rage coloured Curt Lawrence's predatory face.

3

Rimfire Range

TWO boots were hooked over the brass rail. One boot was made by Hyer. The other boot was a Justin. Both boots had run-over heels and were scarred and battered. The Hyer belonged to Tortilla Joe. The Justin boot belonged to Buck McKee.

Tortilla Joe sighed and said to the bartender, "I'll take tequila."

The bartender looked at Buck McKee, a question in his eyes. He was a fat man and his big head was anchored to wide shoulders with a neck as thick as the trunk of a scrub-oak.

"What'll yours be, tall gink?"

"Whiskey," Buck supplied. "Straight, whiteaprons."

The barkeeper lumbered toward the back-bar. He moved with the agility of

35

a sick Hereford bull whose legs were stiff with blackleg. A fat hand went out and wrapped itself around two bottles. These he spun down the polished top of the bar.

The tequila bottle stopped in front of Tortilla Joe.

The whiskey bottle stopped in front of Buck McKee.

Tortilla Joe said, "He ees the expert, no, Buckshots?"

"No," Buck said.

The bartender scowled.

Buck said, "An old trick. Now try it with two glasses."

The fat hand wrapped itself around a glass. This slid down the bar and stopped in front of Buck. The big face wore a happy grin. Another glass slid down the bar and this stopped in front of Tortilla Joe.

Then the bartender looked at Buck. "Now what do you say, hairpin?"

Buck said grudgingly. "All right . . . fer a beginner."

The bartender put his wide back

against the backbar rim. He yawned like a sleepy cougar and slowly closed his eyes. He seemed very tired and very weary; yet, despite this cloak of negligence, Buck McKee seemed to sense an alert vigilance. Sometimes these local bigshots had bartenders staked out as stooges to listen and report back.

Buck glanced at the man. The barkeeper's eyes were closed, his head drooped — but his ears didn't tote ear-plugs.

Buck poured and spoke out of the corner of his mouth. "Speak Mexican, Tortilla," he advised.

Tortilla Joe drank and studied the bartender over the rim of his glass. "Maybe he ees onderstand the Mex?" he said.

The bartender spoke without opening his eyes. "I'm not lissenin' to you damphools yap," he snarled.

"Thanks, pal," Buck returned.

Tortilla Joe suddenly swore at Thick Neck in Mexican. He used some pretty tough words; they rolled off his tongue. Thick Neck studied him in amused indifference. Tortilla Joe added some choice fighting-words. Thick Neck scowled and then went back to his nap, plainly showing no offence at the Mexican's words. Plainly he did not understand the Spanish tongue.

Tortilla Joe said, in Mexican, "He does not understand, Buckshots. Now let us have the long talk, *no es verdad?*"

Buck took another drink. The liquor was a combination of the devil's breath, liquid fire and carbolic acid. He blew on his tongue and grimaced. Tortilla Joe took another snort. His eyes bugged out, his eyes rolled in moist sockets, and he blew and looked down at his breath.

"No see any fire, Buck?"

"Smoke," Buck said, grinning. "No fire, though." The whiskey was eating the varnish off his guts. "This burg has a tough stiff setup, *amigo.*"

Tortilla Joe looked at the front window. A wide window marked by streaks of dust and the markings of houseflies. His face took on a long and pathetic look of suffering.

"The death of his son weel be a hard blow on ol' Sam Perry. Hees only son, Jack was — Eef we had got here only the seconds sooner . . . "

"But we didn't," Buck said practically. He turned his glass slowly and admired the damp rings on the bar. "This Curt Lawrence don't cotton to us, *amigo*. First off, he figures we're gunmen who have come in to side the Perry construction outfit. Second off, he just don't like us 'cause we won't bend to his orders. He's a big shot, Tortilla Joe."

The Mexican nodded. Never one to keep his attention upon a single point or person for any length of time, his mind promptly leaped over the form of big Curt Lawrence and settled on the more pleasing image of a woman, namely one woman named

Clair McCullen.

"That Mees McCullen, now . . . " He sighed with blowing lips. "She ees the beauty, no?"

Buck grunted, "A female hossthief, nothin' more. Operatin' in a rotten town filled with two-bit lynch-mad people . . . But I gotta wait here until she comes back to town with my horse."

"They theenk she breeng een men from Ceenchring Construction, Buckshots. The whole town he ees talk about that. They say there be a beeg fight with the Lawrence outfeet, and the Lawrence *hombre* he ees got gunmen staked out around the town, they tells me."

Buck nodded. "I cain't help but think of poor old Sam Perry, up there in Colorado. His heart will be busted, an' he'll walk on his chin in sorrow. And we gotta notify him, Tortilla."

"We have to send him a *carta*, a letter."

Buck said, "I'm no hand with a pen

or pencil. Can hardly write my own name, 'cept to a cheque payable to me. You'll have to write to Sam, Tortilla Joe."

"But me — I cannot even do the writing, even in the Mexican, Buck. So eet ees up to you, fella."

Thick Neck spoke without opening his eyes. "You two bums are plumb big fools, in my language."

Buck looked at the bartender. "Why them unkind words, fella?"

"You might suddenly find your carcasses weighted down with lead — hot lead, too. Well, if you stick round Buckskin, only one thing I got to say to you."

"And that?" Buck wanted to know.

Thick Neck had his eyes open now. They were wide and sad eyes — they were very, very sad. They had the sad look that a man has when he says good-bye to his bosom friend directly before that beloved friend starts the climb upward to the hangman's noose.

41

"You poor, poor mans," Tortilla Joe murmured, mock sympathy dripping from his words.

"And that one thing?" Buck asked again.

"Good-bye."

Buck grinned. "Thanks."

Thick Neck closed his eyes. His thick chest rose and fell to his measured breathing. To all appearances he was a lizard dozing on a warm rock, at peace with his belly and the world.

Buck paid him no more attention.

Tortilla Joe also had no eyes for the bartender.

Their eyes — rapt and admiring — were on the woman who had sidled between them. Buck saw a small woman not over five feet tall. She was built right in the right places. She had glistening red hair that gleamed and shimmered. Her eyes were green and bright and sharp. Her buckskin blouse, handmade and embroidered with brilliant beads, showed an interesting and rising contour. Her buckskin riding-skirt hugged her full thighs.

Buck said, in awe, "Holy Smoke, and it isn't a doll, either. She's alive, Tortilla Joe." He touched her hand and she did not draw it back. "She's warm and soft, too."

Tortilla Joe stared in make-believe disbelief. "I feel of her other hand." His brown hand went over her tanned hand. His eyes widened. "Hola, alive she ees, sure as the shootin'!"

She did not draw back her hand from the Mexican, either. Her green eyes went from the tall Texan to the squat Mexican. Both held a hand.

Finally she said, "Yes, I'm alive. You can pull back your hands now, men."

Buck grinned. "We ain't been formerly introduced, have we?"

"You mean *formally*, not *formerly*. I have some shocking news for you two bums. Bolster up your knees and prepare for a shock."

"I ready," Tortilla Joe said.

"Me, too," Buck harped in.

The red lips pursed. The green eyes twinkled with mirth. "I am Mrs. Curt Lawrence, gentlemen."

Buck pulled his hand free.

Tortilla Joe pulled back his hand. He looked at Buck and Buck, for the first time, looked away from Mrs. Lawrence.

"Some dogs," mourned Buck, "have all the luck."

She smiled. "Maybe the big wart isn't as lucky as you think, men. The given name is Sybil. Call me by that handle. You're Buck McKee and you're Tortilla Joe something or other . . . That right?"

"Keerect," Buck said.

She studied Buck coldly. "Where are your manners, Sonny Boy? A man should always tend to the wants of the women first, you know."

Buck came back to earth with a start. "Name yore poison, Mrs. Lawrence," he said grandly.

"Whiskey, bartender. Straight, as usual."

She drank the liquid fire with one gulp. She had a handful of diamonds, Buck saw. She tossed the drink down and Buck suddenly winced, remembering his own burning belly. He studied her ears. She caught his glance and a look of surprise came across her little face.

"Why look at my ears, stupid?"

"Lookin' to see if any flame or smoke was comin' outa them," Buck said. "My left big toe is dislocated from that last snort I had from the same bottle."

"Hope it hurts bad," she said dryly.

Buck looked down at her. "You're a runt and Curt Lawrence is a big gent. Never the trains shall meet, or somethin' like that."

She shrugged pretty shoulders. "He's big in body . . . and sometimes too big across the levis. Somebody should take him down a size or two. Sometimes his hat is too small." She looked at Thick Neck. "You got tears in your eyes. Hope they're not for me;

I don't want them. This time pour me a double shot, bartender."

The bottle hit the rim of the glass. The glass went up, met her pretty lips, and the glass came down . . . empty. Buck's big toe on his right foot hurt suddenly. Tortilla Joe said, "I'll watch her ears thees time, Buck."

Sybil Lawrence looked at him. "You're not watching my ears, bucko. Your gaze is down below my neck a little bit."

Buck laughed.

Sybil laughed.

Tortilla Joe blushed like a schoolboy on his first date. He choked on his tequila. He sprayed tequila like a walrus coming up for air. Buck kept on laughing, but now there was conjecture in him. What the heck kind of wife did the curly wolf Curt Lawrence own, anyway? Drinking with two strangers who had run against Lawrence . . . He remembered the terrible, hate-filled look on the big man's face when he had looked down at the twenty-buck gold piece Buck had knocked from his hand. Looked at the gold piece, there in the liquid Arizona dust.

Buck spoke in slow solemness. "If I had a wife, I'd be danged if I'd let her hang around saloons, gabbing with strange and tough men."

The green eyes swung to him. They touched him in cynical appraisal. There was more to this woman than mere bantery, Buck realized. He got this impression and held on to it, and later he found his first guess had been correct. A touch of mockery formed on the pretty lips.

"You aren't married, McKee?"

"Had a wife once, but she run off with a drummer," Buck lied. "She liked his new suitcase."

Her lids were down thoughtfully. "Wonder what kind of a beau you'd make?" she mused.

Buck grinned. "Try me out, honey?"

Suddenly she was serious. "Let's drop this distasteful talk, gentlemen. Marriage, so they say, is an institution.

47

Another definition of an institution is a place where they put loco people . . . I'll lay the facts before you two saddle-warped sinners — you are both up to your Stetsons in trouble!"

Buck glanced at Tortilla Joe. The Mexican's dark eyes were dark fathomless pools of conjecture. Buck thought, What is this leading up to, anyway? But he gave the thought no tongue, waiting for Sybil Lawrence to clarify her statement. Which she soon did.

"My husband is ornery. He's mad at you two, too. First you kept him from catching that Clair McCullen heifer, when she headed for Cinchring to get help to keep the — er, citizens — from hanging Jack Perry. Then, you slapped good money out of his hand, McKee."

"Blood money," Buck murmured.

"Maybe so, McKee. But the whole town watched and saw, and he's got pride — that's one thing the son of cattle king Lawrence — shot down two days ago by Jack Perry — has, gentlemen. You smashed that pride, McKee. And you'll pay through the nose, unless you jerk stakes off this Hammerhead range."

"He doesn't own the air," Buck reminded.

"Maybe he doesn't, but he thinks he's got a deed to it. His old man ran this range the way he saw fit — like a king — and his son has the same idea. Which brings us around to a dead man, one Jack Perry."

Buck realized there was quite a bit here he did not understand. Cinchring Camp, he judged, was the irrigation camp. Therefore it would be composed of muleskinners and fresno-men. He glanced out the window. Lawrence gunhands moved back and forth on Buckskin's main street. This town was a dynamite cache . . . and a big one. If a construction hand rode into town, the match would be dropped . . . Tortilla Joe's voice cut into Buck's unhappy thoughts.

"We never had the honour of meeting Jack Perry, when he was alive."

She frowned. "That's odd. Jack spread word around that two gunmen were being sent down by his father, who is up in Colorado. Those gunmen aimed to help him fight the Hammerhead spread, so he boasted."

Buck groaned.

Tortilla Joe groaned.

Buck said, "Look, Sybil, look. We're jes' dumb, common everyday citizens. We're taxpayers — that's always good for an argument, you know — and we're home lovers, too . . . if we had homes to love . . . Last summer we punched cows for Jack Perry's good old father. A fine man, good to his help. Sam asked us to drop in and say hello to his son. He wrote the son and told him we were coming. He didn't write — the cook did — rheumatiz has the old man's hands crippled. We rode this way to meet the son and *boom* — smack into trouble. We wanted to talk to the son . . . but the son couldn't talk. That's the deal, so help me hanner."

Green eyes touched him. They were girlish and young and yet, back of their exterior, glistened something jade-coloured and strong. Again, Buck glimpsed this; again, he did not like his thoughts.

"That's the gospel truth, huh?"

Tortilla Joe said, "Look, I cross myself."

Buck said, "The whole setup, honey."

Tortilla Joe asked, "What ees thees Ceenchreeng Camp, Meesus Lawrence?"

"Cinchring Creek is north-east of here. Jack Perry had a dirt-moving crew working there. He's building a dam on Hammerhead range. That gal you ran into — "

"She runs eento me," Tortilla Joe corrected. "Hola, weeth her horse, she knocks me an' my horse down, she does. She ees lovely, no?"

"I don't think she's pretty," Sybil Lawrence said sourly. "Kind of a comely wench if you ask me . . . which

51

nobody has. Well, this McCullen woman is the local seamstress — she and Jack Perry were — well, engaged. When they dragged Jack out to lynch him, she headed out for his construction men."

Buck had dreamy eyes as he remembered the loveliness of Clair McCullen. "Too bad Jack got hung," he said thoughtfully. "With her he'd have had an interesting life, to say the least."

"So you might think." The green eyes went from one man to the other. "Which leads us to a pressing question — what are you two sons of Satan doing in Buckskin? The road out of town, gentlemen, is clear."

Buck glanced at Tortilla Joe. "She's been sent by her big husband to warn us," he told his partner

"She ees a female spy, no, Buckshots?"

"Yes."

Sybil Lawrence scowled at them and took another drink. "Both of you are simple damned fools." She spoke next to Thick Neck. "This hooch of yours is getting weak. You got the barrel too close to the town pump!" Again she spoke to the partners. "My husband is out to nail your hides to his corral. And he'll do it if you persist in walking around town, being a red flag in his face — "

She never got to finish her sentence. From behind them came a harsh, danger-filled voice — the voice of an angry man.

"Sybil, get t'hell outa here, savvy! And move pronto, too!"

Buck paused, glass rising. Tortilla Joe's fingers stopped turning his tequila glass. The green eyes of Sybil Lawrence glistened with metallic anger.

All three turned.

Curt Lawrence stood behind them.

4

The Gun Riders

AGAIN, Buck got the impression of bigness. And again with this was another element — anger. Curt Lawrence's craggy face was mean-looking. His lips were wry with anger. He looked at Buck. Cold eyes, mean eyes — the eyes of a ruthless man. Buck got the full measure of their wrath. They did not scare the tall Texan; rather, their insolence slightly angered him. No matter how big a man was in life — or imagined he was — earth levelled him off. That was part of Buck's philosophy. He did not realize this as a philosophy. Time levelled all things — the earth, man, beast, plants. No man was a big man, Buck realized. He just *thought* he was big.

The eyes went to Tortilla Joe. By now shock had left the Mexican and his jowls were simple and full, hanging like the jowls of a hungry and peaceful St. Bernard dog. And the eyes of the Mexican were liquid sadness.

"Get out, wife!"

Still, Sybil did not move. She still stood between the partners.

Buck said, "We don't aim to lead her astray, Lawrence." His voice dripped sarcasm. "We was kinda amused at her talk, figgerin' all the time you had sent her to warn us and to feel us out."

"I fight my own battles," Lawrence said. "I stomp my own snakes. I build my own trail. No woman fights for me, men."

Buck noticed that two men stood behind Curt Lawrence. Gun riders, both of them — the mark of the six-shooter was on them, and its Cain-like brand was for all to see, and thereby judge them. Two guns on each, tied low to bole-like hips. And those dull and deadly gunman eyes . . .

"Get out of here," Curt Lawrence said.

Still, Sybil Lawrence did not move. Two huge strides brought the young cowman forward. His spur rowels made harsh sounds. His big right hand went out and found his wife's small shoulder. He twisted her and she yelped. Then his left hand pushed her.

She went staggering backward. Arms flailing, she cursed him, and her face was twisted with hate. She went into the arms of one of her husband's bodyguards, who held her in a hold.

Lawrence spoke to Buck. "I'm telling you to leave her alone, savvy. And I'm telling you two to hightail out of my town. Right now, too."

Buck said, "Here's my answer!"

Already the lanky cowpoke's right fist was rising. It was coming up in solid and quick determination. His knuckles smashed in Curt Lawrence's jaw. His fist slammed back the big arrogant head. Lawrence snarled something, and Buck's left clipped short his words. The left dropped the Hammerhead *primero*. It dropped him neatly and with final dispatch. It had all happened so fast, and with such cold conciseness, that the big man was also surprised, in addition to being stunned.

Lawrence fell in a sitting down position. He was groggy and the fight, for the moment, had been knocked out of him. Twice in one day this lanky cowpuncher had shamed him and had out-bested him.

Hurriedly, Buck glanced at the two gun riders. But he had no danger there. The one who held Sybil Lawrence stared with his mouth open, surprise etched on his homely face. Buck glanced at the other. To see him he had to look down at the floor. For the man was sprawled on his face, and he was unconscious.

Buck glanced at Tortilla Joe. The Mexican had his .45 out but he still stood with his back to the bar.

"I no slog heem, Buckshots. Thet man, he do eet weeth hees war club."

Buck stared at the newcomer. The newcomer had come in behind the gunman and had dropped him. He was a total stranger to Buckshot McKee. He was one of the oddest specimens of humanity Buck had ever seen in his travels . . . and he had travelled plenty far in his twenty-six years.

"Holy Smoke," he grunted.

The man was short, very short. He was a skinny, desertdried hunk of orneryness. Greasy buckskin trousers were skin tight on skinny legs. On his feet he had moccasins — beady and black with dirt. Above the waist he was naked. He had a scrawny brown chest.

His head, though, was huge.

Buck stared at the immense head, Stringy black hair lay against the huge head, and around the forehead was a wide buckskin thong. His right hand held a heavy Indian war club.

Buck thought. Is he a sideshow freak? He did not put this question into words though, and he gasped, "Thanks for the boost, stranger."

The skinny man lifted his club in front of his face. His lips pursed and he blew on the hardwood. "Don't mention it, Mr. McKee. It was indeed a deep and lasting pleasure. I am, sir, the editor of the local newspaper, lovingly called the *Cactus*."

"A . . . editor?"

"Yes, the man with the blue pencil, sir." He looked down at the unconscious man. "For some time I have yearned to knock this son of hell ice cold. The time finally came. His name, sir, is Will March. When he comes to, anger will be with him — he will undoubtedly reach for his gun, for he will want to kill me." The lips formed a soft sigh, and the pain of living was on the huge face. "This is indeed a cruel and bestial world, Mr. McKee."

Tortilla Joe could only gawk. The gunman released Mrs. Lawrence who went to a chair and sat down. Thick Neck stared, eyes wide open now. The gunman stood undetermined, his courage gone as he looked at Tortilla Joe's big .45 pistol.

Lawrence groaned, head still down.

The editor said, "The name, sir, is Jones — Sitting Bull Jones. One of the Jones' boys, no less. I scouted for General Nelson A. Miles when he tangled with the Sioux up in Montana, therefore my gallant nom de plume." The war club swung out and designated Curt Lawrence. "There sits, sirs, the Royal Nibs, the Crown Prince of Hammerhead Range. Evidently His Honour wants to say a few intelligent words. From this angle, even to my untutored and ignorant eyes, this seems apparent. But for some reason, his huge jaw seems to be reluctant to move, or am I wrong?"

Tortilla Joe said sadly, "You have the good eyes, Seetin' Bull. Thees crown princess, she should not manhandle a woman, no?"

Buck studied Curt Lawrence. The man was gingerly getting to his feet.

Buck's knuckles ached . . . on both hands, too.

Buck said, "She's your wife, Lawrence. From what I'd say, right off-hand, you got a house full of hell in her. Still, she's a woman, even if she is married to a thing like you. And being a woman, she demands a woman's respect. Am I right on that angle, you high-ridin' son of Satan?"

Lawrence spat blood. He looked at Buck in silence. His quiet glance held a raw and livid anger. He looked at Tortilla Joe's naked .45. He turned and looked at the gunman Sitting Bull Jones had buffaloed. Then he walked over to the fallen man. Buck watched, wondering what plan the big cowman had in mind.

Lawrence looked at the man. Cynicism touched him, driving him to anger. His right boot swung back, then ahead. He kicked the unconscious man in the face. He kicked him four times. Two teeth skidded out and became lost in the sawdust. Then Lawrence stepped back, sanity coming to his eyes again.

Sitting Bull Jones chided him with, "Bad, bad little boy, Lawrence. Isn't cricket to kick your little playmate when he is down cold, you know . . . "

Boom . . .

Sybil Lawrence had got her right hand free. She had just slapped the gunman on the jaw. The report sounded like a pistol report. Her open hand left a vivid mark across the gunman's face. Anger flared in his eyes.

"Let her go," Lawrence ordered.

"With pleasure," the gunman said hurriedly.

Hurriedly the gunman released Sybil. Then he rubbed his stubby nose. He got blood on his hand and he looked at it. Her fingernails had ripped the hide off the bridge of his nose.

Lawrence spoke angry words to the gunman. "When Will March comes to tell him to get to hell out of Buckskin and off Hammerhead range, and for good — or I'll kill him personally, savvy?"

"I'll tell him, boss."

Lawrence looked at Tortilla Joe, then at Buck McKee. His angry eyes rested on Sitting Bull Jones who returned his glare. Buck noticed that the editor's knuckles were white as he gripped his war club. Then Curt Lawrence stabbed a glance at his wife.

"You've had your little playday in town, woman. By now you're ready to leave for the ranch! Get out of here and do it right pronto, savvy?"

"You can't run me off, you big baboon."

Lawrence's smile was thin. "You get tough with me, you little runt, and across my knee you go. I've paddled your purty behind before this . . . and I ain't too old to repeat the process!"

Sybil Lawrence looked at Buck McKee. "Thanks for slugging the little fellow," she said. "First time any man has knocked him off his feet!"

Then, without warning, the woman turned quickly on a boot heel. Buckskin riding skirt swishing, she went out the door, and they heard her boots move down the plank walk.

Sitting Bull Jones watched Curt Lawrence with a steady glare. Lawrence said, "You an' me ain't done yet, Sittin' Bull."

"You use terrible English," the editor pointed out. "You should have said. *You* and *I*, not *you* an' *me*."

Lawrence grinned, but it was not a mirthful grin. He spoke now to his gunman. "Let's get out of here." The gunman nodded and moved ahead of the Hammerhead owner. Lawrence was in the doorway when Buck spoke.

"What — no threats?" Buck asked.

Lawrence turned and his eyes probed Buck's. They stood there and appraised each other, and tension was an elastic band between them. Thick Neck stood to one side and he seemed bolted to the floor. Sitting Bull Jones had narrowed old eyes, and he still hung on to his war club. Tortilla Joe, seemingly sleepy and dopey, still held his big .45. He held it in a lazy, stupid manner, the barrel pointing down at the floor. Lawrence looked at the naked gun. One movement, and up would come that barrel; a flick of the dark thumb, the hammer would rise and fall. That gun didn't fool Curt Lawrence. This was written plainly on his face. Then he swung his gaze back to Buck McKee.

"Only a fool makes threats, McKee."

"That's right," Buck admitted. "Only a fool . . . "

Lawrence said, "You aim to stick around Buckskin, I take it?"

"We might stay," Buck answered. "We might not stay."

Lawrence nodded, seemingly busy with his thoughts.

"We'll meet again," he promised. He said no more. He went outside. Buck heard his boots pound on the worn and dried-out plank walk. Soon the cowman moved past the window. He walked with determination, and he was big and powerful and tough. Then he moved out of sight and the sound of his bootheels left, too.

"Only a fool . . . " Thick Neck repeated. And his voice held sarcasm. Buck looked at him with a smile.

"You're sand paperin' my patience," Buck told him. "Now don't get me so I don't like you, Thick Neck."

Thick Neck had no reply. He swallowed once, then moved out of reach. He was remembering the rapidity with which Buck had knocked down Curt Lawrence. Thick Neck therefore was prudent.

Buck looked down at Will March, who was still sound asleep. "You don't figure you done caved in his skull for keeps, do you, Sittin' Bull?"

The old printer went to one bony knee. Ink-stained fingers found Will March's wrist. He cocked his huge head and there was a silence, then the editor got to his feet. He brushed sawdust off his knee.

"Heart as solid and strong as a grandfather clock, Buck."

Tortilla Joe said, "A rider, he ees come."

66

They listened and the hoofs came closer. The rider was loping down the main street. Tortilla Joe listened again.

"Only one rider," he said.

Buck said, "Thought mebbe the Cinchring bunch was coming into town. Thought mebbe the fireworks would break loose."

They kept watching the window. Soon the rider would move into view. The hoofs came closer. Tortilla Joe watched, Buck watched, and Sitting Bull Jones watched. Thick Neck dozed. Will March slept peacefully.

Then, the rider came into view. The horse was rimmed with sweat, and plainly the bronc was dog-tired from a long ride. Buck said, "My bronc," and then he looked at the rider.

"Clair McCullen," he said.

5

Bullet Trail

THEY went outside. Buck in the lead, Tortilla Joe second, and Sitting Bull Jones taking up the rear, war club and all. By this time Clair McCullen had dismounted. She had tears in her eyes and her lips trembled in anger.

"You two — still around?"

Buck shrugged, spread his hands. "Had to wait for my horse," he supplied. "I could swear out a warrant and jail you for stealin' my bronc, you know. We're friends of a man we've never seen, now lynched. Worked up in Colorado last summer for Jack's dad, old Sam Perry."

"You did! I'm sorry about taking your horse — I had to get out to Cinchring camp — "

Buck asked, "What happened out there?"

She leaned against the hitch-rack, sobbing. The whole town of Buckskin watched. They stood on the street and watched and hid behind windows and watched. A Lawrence gunman moved in to listen.

Buck said, "Get t'hell outa here, gundog!"

The man stood there, studying Buck with a cynical grin. His hand was on his .45. Buck moved towards him. Tortilla Joe twirled his gun on his forefinger. Sunlight flashed off the barrel.

"Okay," the gunman said, "okay. Don't get hot under the collar, people."

He walked away. Buck grinned. He turned his attention to the weeping girl. He got the impression that this girl had really loved Jack Perry. This was a bitter, terrible day for her. His heart went out to her in her grief. And when he spoke his voice was low with emotion.

"Tell us, Miss Clair."

"Those construction hands — they wouldn't believe me — They said Jack was safe in jail, that the Hammerhead would never dare lynch him. They wouldn't head back with me, the cowards . . . "

Buck waited. Tortilla Joe waited. Sitting Bull Jones rubbed his eyes. Sitting Bull Jones said, "Wind . . . always makes my eyes water." Sitting Bull Jones was lying. He knew it. Tortilla Joe knew it. Buck McKee knew it, also.

"I begged them to ride into Buckskin and save Jack. Then a man rode out to camp — he told them Jack was already lynched — I should kill that Curt Lawrence, just like Jack killed his old man!"

Buck said, "They showed wisdom."

She glared at him. "Wisdom? What do you mean, you fool? Their boss — the man who foots their payroll — he got lynched! They aren't even men enough for fight for their outfit!"

Buck nodded patiently. "Curt Lawrence had this town spiked with guns, Clair.

Him and his Hammerhead hands are just hoping those dirt men will ride in. Then they can wipe out the whole dirt camp and the fight will be over, with Lawrence and his Hammerhead the winner."

"I'll — I'll kill him."

Her voice was savage. She was either in sorrow, or either a competent actress. Buck suddenly grabbed her by the right wrist.

"Come with me, woman!"

She stared at him, tears glistening in her eyes. Surprise had instantly taken the place of rage and sorrow.

"What do you want, Mister?"

"You stole my bronc. They hang people for stealin' horses, you know. The best place for you is in the county jail!"

"Jail!" Her voice showed she doubted his sanity. "I brought your horse back, didn't I?"

"Come along with me."

Buck pulled her after him. She did not resist very long. She trotted along, with Tortilla Joe behind her, with Sitting Bull Jones behind the Mexican. And with the town of Buckskin watching and wondering.

"Where we going?" she panted.

"To talk to the sheriff," Buck replied.

"Why — the sheriff?"

Buck did not answer. She did not see the wink he sent Tortilla Joe. The thought had come to the tall Texan that the longer this girl stayed in circulation the sooner she would get into trouble. She might even try to kill Curt Lawrence. She would be better off behind bars, he had reasoned. But he did not tell her this. It was a rough deal all the way around.

The sheriff had a small log office. He sat down behind a table that held various items: old western story magazines, two worn-down law books, a rifle and an old scattergun. When they came in his boots were on the desk, too. Spur rowels were digging into the battered top. New boots they were, highly polished, glistening. Buck thought of his old battered boots. Maybe a man should settle down, get a soft county job, and get new boots every two months?

He was a short man, this sheriff, and he had an enormous belly. He had a bald head that glistened like a billiard ball smeared with lard. Long handlebar moustaches hung down on each side of his thick-lipped mouth and his eyes were big and watery. He looked like he had about as much backbone as a jellyfish.

"What's the commotion about?" the lawman wanted to know.

"This gal," said Buck, "stole my bronc."

Clair McCullen tried to jerk away unsuccessfully. She still didn't know whether Buck was drunk or crazy . . . or a combination of both.

"Let go of me," she stormed.

Buck said, "You sure got a nice arm, honey."

The sheriff let his new boots hit the floor with a thud. His watery eyes studied Buck, went to the girl, flicked to Tortilla Joe, then landed on Sitting Bull Jones. They studied the big-headed editor and his war club. Evidently these two did not have too much mutual affection.

Then the lawman said, "She brought your horse back, McKee."

Buck nodded. "That she did. But remember, lawman, she had to steal it first, or she couldn't have brought it back."

Clair McCullen had stopped struggling. Buck let his hand slide down her wrist and he squeezed her little hand. She glared at him with cold indifference.

"You dirty louse! All you want to do is hold my hand. That's why you're creating this scene!"

"My, my," Buck chortled. "What a lively imagination."

Tortilla Joe's dark eyes were roving around the room. Then finally they settled in sadness on the pot-bellied sheriff.

"What ees your name, starman?"

"Potter, Henry Potter. You two, they tell me, is Buck McKee and Tortilla Joe." He looked at Buck again. "I can't hold this woman."

Buck tried another angle. "She threatened to try to kill Curt Lawrence," he told Potter.

Potter came instantly awake. "She did! Well, that's different — a threat to kill is far greater than a charge of stealing a horse." His watery eyes narrowed in sudden thought. "How come you're so careful of the well-being of Curt Lawrence, McKee?"

"File the complaint, and shut up."

The lawman's eyes glistened, despite their moistness. He plainly did not like the tall Texan's authoritative tone of voice. But he said, "All right, after I take her to a cell. Come along, woman."

Clair McCullen planted both little feet solidly against the worn pine floor. The lawman got her by both arms and dragged her out the door and they heard him pull her down the cell aisle. Buck glanced back into the cell department. Potter was just slamming the door shut on Clair McCullen.

"Why did you jail her?" Tortilla Joe asked.

Buck grinned. "A night in the clink will sober her up. She'll be mad when she comes out but she won't act on impulse. By then the edge of her grief will be worn off. Come tomorrow I aim to drop the charges."

"Good idea," Sitting Bull Jones chimed in.

Sheriff Potter ambled back and he almost pushed his chair through the floor, he sat down so suddenly and so hard. He took out an old blue bandana and tried to rub the sweat off his greasy forehead, but the sweat popped out right behind the dirty handkerchief.

"I've had a tough, rough day," the lawman lamented.

Buck studied him. "I don't see how you did have, if you want the blunt truth. They lynched a man in this town today. A lynching is against the law — direct violation of the law books."

Potter's thick lips trembled in anger. "McKee, watch your big mouth! This peaceful town don't like trouble makers. My prisoner was delivered out of jail by a mob — all masked — "

"Why didn't you stop them?" Buck asked.

Potter bent down to show his bald head. "I was slugged, knocked cold. Wrapped over the head with a club. No wonder my head has a splittin' headache! I never identified a one of the lynchers. All masked. If Curt Lawrence hadn't been out chasing that female, I'd have jugged him as one of them. But he was out in the desert — "

"Maybe that's why he was out there," Buck said.

Potter studied him. "Explain that statement, bucko?"

Buck spread his hands. "Maybe Lawrence didn't want to catch the girl. Maybe he used his chasin' her as an alibi to get out of town while his other men, masked and ugly, pulled a man out of a cell and lynched him? By chasing her he was in the clear."

"Them is harsh words, McKee."

Buck shrugged. "Could be true."

Potter studied him with unblinking eyes. Buck sensed a hardness permeate this thick man, and he realized Potter was getting madder by the moment. Buck decided to quit deviling him.

"You two fellas have caused a lot of trouble today. Twice you insulted Curt Lawrence."

"Only once," Buck corrected. "The first time I insulted him. That was when I knocked that gold piece outa his hand. The second time I didn't insult him — I just knocked him on his rump."

"Then you knocked out one of his gun — Er, his men, they tell me."

Sitting Bull Jones said, "He didn't do that — I did. With my little club." He kissed the war club, lips making a *smacking* sound. "My little war club and I."

Buck tried something. "Did Curt Lawrence come in here and want a complaint filed against us?"

"No . . . The Hammerhead fights its own battles, McKee."

Buck nodded. "Yes, and the Hammerhead apparently lynches its enemies, too. Even takes them out of the county jail to string them up, too . . ."

"They slugged me cold!"

"I forgot that," Buck said.

Potter leaned his bulk forward. The spring on his swivel chair howled in oilless protest. He did not seem angry. He seemed fatherly and benevolent suddenly. His fat forefinger jabbed a hole in the air.

"McKee, you two are in trouble. You don't hit a man like Lawrence . . . and live. That goes for you, too, editor. You slugged a Lawrence man. You three got two things to do. One is to stay here . . . and stop breathing; the other, to drift out and forget this whole nasty affair. That clear?"

"Sure is," Buck said.

"Like the mud," Tortilla Joe said.

Sitting Bull Jones had a long lonesome look. "I got too much invested to pull out and leave," he mourned.

Sheriff Potter leaned back. Again the spring protested. "That's the size of the deal," the lawman said.

"Thanks," Buck said.

"*Gracias*," Tortilla Joe said.

Sitting Bull Jones bowed in grandiose manner. "My friend, many thanks for the fatherly warning." He straightened, face deadpan. "It shall be heeded, also. Again, thanks."

They trooped out then. Sitting Bull in the lead, Tortilla Joe in the middle, and gangling Buck McKee taking up the rear. Behind them Sheriff Henry Potter chewed the end of one handlebar moustache and watched and wondered just who had made a fool out of whom.

They stopped and gave attention to the sunset. The sinking sun had lost its heat, but heat danced out of the sand. Somewhere a sagebrush bloomed, its aroma sweet. Buck thought, only nice thing in this town, and let it go at that. Then the thought came that he had met something nicer than the desert aroma. Clair McCullen. She'd be a nice one to hold and hug, he decided. Yes, and Sybil Lawrence — she was a well-built dish, too.

Tortilla Joe said, "That sheriff, he ees no get the slogged. He bend over an' hees head — she has no marks. No bruises. He ees the beeg liar, Buckshots."

"Lawrence man," Buck grunted.

Tortilla Joe yawned. "We get the bunks for thees night an' when the sun he comes up we dreeft for Yuma, no? Nobody she testify against Clair — she be free — "

Buck said, "Bet you twenty bucks I kiss her before we leave."

"I take that."

Sitting Bull said, "I'm gonna go to my shop. Get out my sheet. Drop in when you walk by. Right down the street, men."

He hurried away. Buck watched him go and smiled. The world was full of odd characters. Then the thought came that maybe he was one himself, and his smile died.

Sitting Bull Jones disappeared in a door.

"We leave come the daylights, Buckshots?"

Buck looked at the squat Mexican. "What about Jack Perry?"

"He ees the dead, lynched. What about heem?"

"He's the only son of old Sam Perry, remember?"

"I know that."

Buck spoke softly. "We punched cows for old Sam. He treated us like we was his own flesh and blood."

"I think . . . of that, *tambien*."

Buck grinned. "Hades, partner, you're way behind time — the train left an hour ago."

"What do you means by that, Buckshots?"

Buck spread his long fingers.

"Simple . . . Curt Lawrence couldn't afford to let us ride out of this country scot-free . . . Talk is going around about the two drifters that knocked Lawrence down and showed him up in front of all these people. They've lived in fear of the Hammerhead for years. Lawrence has to keep up his rep as a tough gent. We couldn't ride out if we wanted to. Do you want to pull out?"

Tortilla Joe shook his head. "No, *señor*," he said.

"Then close your big mouth."

They went down the street. They came to an adobe building. A door sagged on its hinges in dejection. From the unlit interior came the booming voice of Sitting Bull Jones.

"Come in, *compadres*, come in. *Entrez vous*, hombres."

They went inside. The interior was gloomy. No candle or lamp was lighted. The place smelled of mice, paper, ink and oil. A handpress made a metallic sound. Sitting Bull Jones stood in front of a type case picking out type. He wore a long leather apron — so long he almost stepped on it when he came to meet Buck and Tortilla Joe.

"You so poor you can't afford to buy coal oil?" Buck asked. "Dark as a tomb in here and stinks twice as much."

"You ever been in a tomb?" the old man countered. He did not wait for an answer. "We have to keep it dark. Somebody shot at us through the window the other night. Lawrence bunch, we're sure. So . . . no lights. When it gets too dark, we quit working. Ain't that right, helper?"

The helper grinned toothlessly and nodded. He was working a hand press and Buck doubted if he had heard a word his boss had said. All his skinny weight would go forward against the lever. The old press was as noisy as an approaching earthquake. The heavy stamp lifted, hesitated, then fell with a clanging noise. A skinny Mexican boy, naked except for torn pants, fed paper into the press.

Sitting Bull Jones shook hands with the partners. Evidently he was of the handshaking fraternity. He acted as though he had not seen Buck and Tortilla Joe for years. He fairly pulled Buck over to the press. He got one of the sheets of paper and held it under the cowpuncher's nose.

His voice held triumph. "Read that headline, McKee."

Buck read aloud.

MCKEE BEATS HELL OUT OF LAWRENCE;
KNOCKS HIM DOWN!

Sitting Bull Jones chuckled. He sounded as happy as a squirrel who had just discovered a shiny new walnut under some leaves. His eyes were the sharp eyes of a gopher as he studied Buck's weather-beaten face.

"What do you think of it, McKee?"

Buck put the paper on the bench. "Curt Lawrence will hang your hide on to his bunkhouse wall when that extra hits the streets, Sittin' Bull. You're rubbin' his fur the wrong way an' you're using a hard curry-comb to do it."

"We print the truth," the old man said, beaming. "The whole truth an' nothin' but the truth."

Tortilla Joe got philosophical. "Some times they keel mens for tellin' the truth."

The press had stopped. The toothless printer gawked at them. The Mexican boy watched them. Buck got the impression that he and Tortilla Joe were as odd in this town as a white man is on Mars. They had gone against the Crown Prince and were still alive, too . . .

Buck said, "It will get Lawrence even madder at us, too."

Sitting Bull Jones let words tumble from his lips. "Are you two men cowards?" Again, he waited for no answer. "Let me tell you buckos a bit of delicate information. This might shock your sweet little constitutions so brace yourself. Curt Lawrence has issued orders, men — orders, get me?"

"As to what effect?" Buck wanted to know.

The old man watched; the Mexican gawked. Tortilla Joe said nothing. Outside the dust thickened. Somewhere a dog barked and somewhere children played. They called in Mexican to each other.

"His men are to pen you in on Hammerhead range, McKee. You can't ride out of this area. When you knocked him down in the saloon, you did more than hammer him on the jaw — you hit him in his pride."

Buck nodded. "Figgered that." He started for the door. Again, the words of the old publisher halted him.

"McKee, a moment."

"Yeah?"

"Will March, the gent I knocked cold. There's talk around, McKee. Curt Lawrence dressed him down with his tongue, and laid it to him — so they tell me."

Buck said, "March should be mad

at you, not me. You was the one what chilled him with your club."

"Watch him, Buck."

Tortilla Joe asked, "Who keel ol' John Lawrence, Seetin' Bull? Jack Perry, he keel Curt's father?"

Sitting Bull eagerly went into action. Nobody knew for sure who had shot down the old cattle king. He had been found dead, shot through and through, out on the desert, just south of the Cinchring construction camp.

"Sheriff Potter, he found some empty cartridge cases. The firing-pin had landed on them in a peculiar manner."

"Yeah?" Buck said.

The sheriff had taken Jack Perry's Winchester .30-30. He had fired it about a hundred times. Each time the firing-pin landed on the cartridge case just as had the firing-pin that had exploded the cartridges that had killed John Lawrence.

Buck grunted, "All circumstantial evidence, eh?"

"What Jack Perry he say in hees deefense?" Tortilla Joe asked.

"He claimed he didn't kill the old cowman. He said he had two Winchester rifles, both .30-30 calibre. I talked a long time with him. He said one of them was stole from him. Taken from the construction camp. Gone for a few days and then suddenly was on the rack again. This was the rifle that shot old John. Of course, suspicion immediately pointed toward Jack, because he and John Lawrence had had a couple of arguments."

Buck rubbed his long jaw thoughtfully. "If Jack Perry didn't kill the cowman, who did kill him?"

"Nobody knows, Buck," the editor returned.

Tortilla Joe shrugged. Buck McKee shrugged. They went outside. The last light of day rimmed the far scarp mountains. Suddenly, Buck stopped. He stared between two buildings into the alley.

"You see somebody — sometheengs?"

Tortilla Joe demanded.

Buck said quietly, "A woman just sneaked into that door we see back there. The door to that brick building, Tortilla. She went in fast, too — she didn't want anybody to see her. By accident I glimpsed her."

"Who was she?"

"Sybil Lawrence."

6

Rendezvous

TORTILLA JOE stared at the door. He spoke in a quiet voice. "That door she ees the back door of the bank, eet looks to thees son of Sonora, Buck. What ees wrong with her going into the bank, even eef by the back door?"

"She sneaked in there. She didn't want anybody to see her. And why would she sneak in?"

The Mexican lifted his heavy shoulders. "I not know." He let his shoulders fall. "We go back eento the alley, no?"

"Yes."

They travelled between the two buildings, heading for the alley. Tortilla Joe could hardly squeeze through the space but Buck walked along easily in the narrow confine. They came to the alley with its tin cans and garbage and its dust. They were at the rear of the brick bank, and Buck sidled close to a barred window. A lamp was lit inside the bank and the blind was pulled low. Buck squatted and squinted under the blind. He whistled softly as he watched. Tortilla Joe got on his knees and looked under the blind, too.

"Well, I'll be the dog that was goned," the Mexican murmured.

A man and a woman were in the room. Evidently it was the banker's office. They stood in the middle of the room. Sybil Lawrence stood on tiptoe, arms around the man's neck. She was kissing him fervently and long. Shamelessly the partner's watched.

"She kees heem long time," Tortilla Joe muttered.

Buck asked, "You jealous?"

"She can kees me any time she wants, Buck."

Buck grinned. "That ain't Curt Lawrence she's swappin' spit with,

either. Good lookin' gent, whoever
he is. Well, we know one thing, for
what it's worth — if worth anything."

"*Si?*"

"She's not faithful to the Curly Wolf.
Hey, get down — pronto — "

With a sweep of his arm, he sent
Tortilla Joe to the dust. Up ahead in
the alley Buck had caught the last rays
of the sun flashing on a rifle barrel.
The rifleman was crouching behind a
wooden garbage barrel. Sunlight had
drifted through between two buildings
to flash from his rifle barrel.

Tortilla Joe grunted, "What een the
heck — ?"

Buck was on one knee, short gun
out. The rifle spouted lead. The man
missed because of Buck's sudden slip
to one knee. Buck's .45 talked, flames
spouting out of the barrel. All the time,
above the roar of rifle and short gun,
he remembered old Sitting Bull Jones'
prophecy.

Buck shot through the edge of the
wooden barrel. Above the pound of

his .45 he heard a man's high pitched scream. The man staggered out from behind his protection. His rifle hit the dust, slid to one side, stopped.

The man's knees sprang out. He fell on his belly, head buried in the dust. Buck got to his boots, knees shaky. Tortilla Joe got up and brushed dust from him. The Mexican's jowls were chalk white.

"Ambush . . . " he murmured. "Dirty range, ambush range . . . "

They walked ahead, with Buck shoving new cartridges into his cylinder. The town had jerked itself awake. People hollered, kids screamed, dogs barked. Even a burro took up the noise by braying in a doleful manner. Buck toed the man over and stared down at his dead ugly face.

Will March would never kill another man.

Buck said, "Lawrence sent him against me, Tortilla Joe. We don't leave this range, friend, until this is settled."

"I say okay to that, Buckshots."

People were converging down on them. They were gawking at the dead man. Buck had hit him three times in the chest. They were admiring the bullet-holes, for they covered a small area. Sheriff Potter came on the run. His run was a slow, animal dog-trot. His bald head glistened. He stared at the dead man, then at Buck, then at Tortilla Joe.

"What — what happened, men?"

Buck told him.

The lawman stabbed a glance at Tortilla Joe. "Will you verify that version, Mexican?"

Tortilla Joe knew what *verify* meant, but he played ignorant. He shrugged and spread his hands and a look of stupidity coloured his jowls. "I know not what you mean, lawmans."

"Is that true?"

"Oh, sure, that ees the truth. Like Buckshots says, lawmans — that ees the right truth."

Buck grinned. "Ask March how it

happened, sheriff?" he taunted.

"Don't rub me the wrong way," growled Sheriff Henry Potter. "Anybody else see the gunfight?"

"Not me," a man said. "I want no part of this."

Nobody volunteered. Potter had two men tote the corpse into the morgue. Buck noticed that Sybil Lawrence was in the crowd. About ten feet from her stood the man she had been kissing in the bank office.

She looked at Buck, green eyes sharp. "You're a handy man with that gun, McKee. Curt won't like this one bit."

Buck said, "That's okay with me, honey. Tell the big lug to come himself the next time. A man who orders an ambush is as low and filthy as the man who carries out the ambush. That makes your loving spouse a low and filthy man."

"He'll rise up in wrath," she said.

Buck looked at the man who had kissed her. He was about thirty, he figured — well built and well dressed and neat. Evidently he shied away from all physical labour. He was a good-looking man, roughly handsome and one who would appeal to women, Buck guessed.

Buck noticed that the man, despite his well-dressed appearance, toted a six-shooter.

"Here comes Curt," a man said.

The gathering split. The Crown Prince of Hammerhead range pushed through. Behind him trailed a gunman. He was the fellow who had jerked Sybil around, when Curt Lawrence had thrown her into his arms. He scowled. Lawrence scowled. There was a deep, deadly silence.

"You killed March, McKee?"

"I did."

"Why?"

"He tried to kill me?"

Buck noticed that Sitting Bull Jones was standing beside Tortilla Joe. The old editor was busy taking down notes on a piece of paper tacked to a wide board.

Lawrence merely nodded. His eyes, though, held a scheming look. "Why would March tie into you, McKee?"

"Your orders, I reckon."

Curt Lawrence watched him. The gunman studied Tortilla Joe. The gnarled and dark hand of Sitting Bull Jones kept on writing. He was making some funny-looking characters on the paper. Buck found out later it was shorthand.

Lawrence seemed to be talking to himself. "This ain't logical. March didn't cross you when we had a ruckus in the saloon. He got knocked cold by old Sitting Bull. I kicked out two of his front teeth myself. Yet . . . he ties into you. Did you and him ever have trouble before . . . on some other range?"

The big man's wide, hard face showed nothing. "Explain yourself, McKee?" he asked quietly.

"You made a deal with March. Paid him to move against my gun. The whole town knows about it."

"Can you prove that?"

"No . . . "

"Then keep your big mouth shut, McKee."

Buck moved towards Lawrence. The cowman stood his ground. His hand was not toying with the gold chinstrap nugget now. His hands were down with his thumbs hooked in his gunbelt and with his fingers splayed over the handles of his guns. But still, his face was deadpan, without expression, without thoughts. Schooled and tough, this man.

Sitting Bull Jones said, "I heard about the talking you handed March, Lawrence. The swamper at the saloon heard it. He blabbed all over town like a lovesick old woman."

"Shut up, you printer's devil!"

Buck said, "Make your play — "

But before either could draw, a man had forced his way between them. He was the well-dressed man whom Sybil Lawrence had kissed in the bank's office. He did not talk to Buck.

He addressed his words to Curt Lawrence.

"Lawrence, don't pull your gun here, please. Some innocent people might get killed. I want to talk to you in my office. Your wife should come along, too. Let this ride for now . . . Curt."

Potter pushed in. "That's right," he said. His sweaty forehead glistened in the twilight. "Hell's bells, will this trouble never stop?"

"Your job is to stop it," a man said.

Potter whirled, enormous bulk turning. He scanned the crowd with bitter eyes. "Who said that?"

Nobody answered. A kid hooted, a woman laughed. Potter spoke again to Lawrence. "Halloway is right. Go with him, Curt."

Lawrence looked at Buck, then at Tortilla Joe, then at Sitting Bull. Suddenly he showed a twisted smile.

"There's always another day," he said.

He and Sybil went towards the back

door of the bank. The man named Halloway spoke to Buck.

"I'm the local banker. Name of Halloway — Martin Halloway. You boys have been in Buckskin only a few hours. Already you have killed a man, you've knocked down Curt Lawrence, and Sitting Bull here knocked out Will March."

Buck said, "What is it to you?"

"I'm a member of this town. An influential member, I might add. Until you came in these people knew peace — "

Buck kept the anger out of his voice. But he clipped his words. "They sure did know peace," he said scornfully. "They're so peaceful they even lynch a man in broad daylight because Lawrence so ordered. Were you one of the killers who was hiding behind a mask, banker?"

The handsome face paled. The lips trembled in anger. Buck saw that this man, despite his well-groomed appearance, was hard and tough underneath. For a moment, he thought that the banker would draw his gun.

Then he saw caution come in and veil the harsher emotions. And the lips of the banker moved slowly.

"We'll find out who slugged the sheriff, McKee. When we do the guilty party — or parties — will pay. We'll find out who's behind the lynching of Jack Perry. Those people will pay, too."

Buck smiled tightly.

Sitting Bull Jones broke into the conversation with, "You'll find them! You'll make them pay! Hogwash of the foulest quality, Halloway. If you arrested them lynchers, maybe you'd have to throw yourself into jail, eh?"

"I wasn't in on it."

"All men look alike with masks on," the old editor said savagely.

The banker looked at him with narrowed eyes. Buck got the idea there was no lost love between these two. Evidently Sitting Bull Jones, because of his sense of fairness and justice, because of his sharp tongue and sharp pen and press, was not too popular in this town of Buckskin.

Halloway said, "Ever since you came to town, Sitting Bull, this town has been in a turmoil. Why the hell don't you move out of here if you don't like the burg?"

"I aim to make it so I can like it, banker. These farmers spell one word, *progress*. They're coming in legally and using legal homestead rights. The Lawrence outfit has tried to run them out since the day they started building their dam. You can't stop progress, you know. Not even greed stops progress."

"I oughta twist your neck around so you can look down your spine!"

Sitting Bull Jones retreated not an inch. He raised his war club and looked at it solemnly. He talked to the club, not to Halloway.

"This club hit a man alongside the head, and it'll knock his head off. That knot in you can scrape the hide off a man's skull. Wonder how this

Shylock would look if you accidentally got bounced off his thick skull? This town is full of accidents you know, War Club. Maybe an accident could happen to this banker?"

Halloway turned and spoke to Sheriff Potter. "That's a threat against my well-being," he snapped. "Arrest this printer bum, sheriff."

"I'm not talking to him," the editor told the lawman. "I was merely talking to my friend, my war club. He had no reason to eavesdrop."

"Right he is," Buck chimed in, grinning.

Potter was caught between the deep freeze and the steam house. Sweat popped out on his face. The crowd was laughing.

"Halloway, go, please," the sheriff said.

Halloway grinned. Buck sensed that the banker realized public opinion was running against him and the longer he stayed in the public eye the higher that opinion would become.

"Hope you two heed me and my advice," he told Buck and Tortilla Joe.

Buck said, "We might . . . and we might not . . . "

"If you have any sense, you will."

Buck shrugged. "Both of us is plumb senseless. Down in Sonora province one time we went to *siesta* in the shade of a mesquite. Mexican goat came along nibbling and eat our brains."

"Chew up all our brains," Tortilla Joe lamented, face long and dour.

"A couple of trigger-happy idiots," the banker spat.

He walked away, heavy with self importance. Somebody started laughing. The banker turned and looked at the man with hard eyes. The man stopped laughing.

"Sorry, Halloway."

Buck noticed that the speaker was an old man, and he seemed crippled in his right leg. He and the banker glared at each other. Potter watched, Buck watched, and Tortilla Joe watched. Sitting Bull Jones sported a wide grin.

"You shouldn't have laughed at Money Bags," Buck told the crippled oldster. "He might foreclose on your mor'gage and turn you out into the cold, cold world. Age means nothing to a banker, you know."

"He ain't no mor'gage on me," the old man said.

The cripple spat largely and hugely. Brown tobacco juice spurted out. Whether he meant to spit on Halloway, or have the sputum land close to him — Buck did not know. But he did know one thing.

The brown stream jetted out to hit Halloway on the left hand. Anger flushed the banker's face and he came rushing towards the cripple, fists doubled. The old man, hurrying to get away, fell down. Halloway grinned savagely and his right boot went back to kick the oldster in the ribs.

The kick never landed.

That was because Buck McKee stepped into the trouble. He used the same twin blows that had dropped

Curt Lawrence. A solid rising left, flush on the button, followed by an overhand right. The next thing Halloway knew was that the ground came up and hit him.

Eyes blurred, blood on his lips, he stared upward at Buck McKee, who still had his fists doubled.

"A man don't hit women, kids or cripples," Buck gritted.

Halloway spat blood. His face still held the dazed, stunned look. Slowly, gingerly, he got to his knees. For a moment he stood like an animal, on all fours. During this interval Tortilla Joe stepped forward and got the banker's gun.

He handed it to Sheriff Potter.

"Keep it safe for the leetle banker boy," the Mexican said scornfully.

Potter held the gun by the barrel. It must have been redhot. He held it awkwardly. He watched the banker get unsteadily to his feet. The banker swung around and looked at the sheriff.

"I demand you arrest this man."

"On what charge?" Potter asked.

"Assault and battery, of course. You saw him hit me, you stupid fat pelican!"

Buck saw a hardness enter the sheriff's hanging jowls. "Don't get rough with me, Halloway. You hold no mor'gage over this boy. You went to kick an old helpless man. I damned near slugged you myself. McKee just beat me to it."

Buck said, "You stumbled over a rock, and fell on it."

Halloway studied the tall cowpuncher. "You gone plumb loco, McKee?"

Buck kicked at a good sized rock. "You fell over that. You clipped your jaw on it."

The old man said, "He sure did, McKee. I seen it."

Banker Halloway had had enough. He pivoted and went into his office. He slammed the door so hard the hinges bounced.

Buck looked at Sheriff Potter.

The sheriff winked.

7

Lawless Grass

BUCK looked at the pretty, dark-haired young waitress. This range, he decided, had some lovely women. Beside him sat Tortilla Joe, dumbly studying a menu. He couldn't read a word of English and darned little Spanish, either.

"What we eat, Buck?"

Buck sighed. He and Sheriff Potter had had a talk. There would be a coroner's inquest over the body of Will March. Two days from now, the sheriff said. The body would keep. A fellow in the town would shoot the veins full of alcohol.

"Not the kind a man drinks," the sheriff had informed. "That other kind what kills him if he gets it in his belly."

"I'm going to my office," Sitting Bull Jones had said.

So now Buck McKee and Tortilla Joe sat in the Greasy Plate Café. At long last they were going to get something to eat. Though neither had much of an appetite. It had been a rough, tough day . . . and maybe it wasn't over yet . . .

Buck remembered Potter's wink. Evidently Banker Halloway and Potter were not such firm friends. He got the idea that they could push the fat sheriff so far, and then hell would pop. Or was he wrong? Potter had seemingly worked in cahoots with the lynchers.

"Darn those kids," the waitress said.

The boys had their noses pressed to the front window. They were hero-worshipping Buck McKee and Tortilla Joe.

The waitress shooed them away.

"I just washed that window today," she informed Buck. "Now they're going to get it all mucked up with their dirty noses." She put their plates in front of them. "You two are sort of town heroes, if you don't know it."

"Heroes they sometimes get keeled," Tortilla Joe said. "Now you make me two more of these *tortillas*, no?"

"You must like them?"

"That ees what ees geeve me my maiden name."

"Not *maiden* name," Buck corrected. "*Given* name, you mean."

"What she ees makes no deeference. As long as they no call me too late for meals, I am happy."

Buck watched the waitress walk back to the kitchen. She had a nice back and nice hips and thin legs. She was built just right, he realized. Well, so was Clair McCullen. He grinned. She was still in jail. Do her good, he figured. Knock her off her high horse a little. Too bad he couldn't get Sybil Lawrence in the same cell with Clair. A jail term would do Sybil good, too. He pondered on this delectable possibility. Finally Tortilla Joe's words, coming around a mouthful of beans, took him back to the present.

"Some theengs they ees rotten here een Arizona Territories, Buckshots."

"Like what?"

"Sybeel, she ees kees thees banker. She ees another man's wife."

Buck grinned. "That ain't nothin' new," he said.

"No theeng, he ees sacred no longer?"

Buck glanced at his partner. For a moment he had taken the Mexican seriously. Then he saw the long and dour look on his partner's face. He jabbed his elbow deep into the fat ribs.

"You ol' Romeo. You've kissed many another man's wife in your time. And don't try to lie out of it, either!"

"That ees the wrong attitude."

More kids pushed their noses against the clean window. Already dirty streaks were beginning to form on the glass.

The waitress came in with the *tortillas*. She was hot and angry and irritable. She kept brushing her hair back. Buck speared a spare hair in his soup. She chased the kids away.

Buck found another hair in his soup.

Matrimony, he thought sourly, was a hell of a mess. Good for married men and women, but not for single drifters. No wonder the human race was disintegrating so quickly — fools got married, and only fools. Suddenly he had a vision of Clair McCullen. Dark and small and lovely — even prettier when those lovely eyes flashed in anger.

She was plenty mad, in that cell.

The waitress came back from chasing away another bunch of young fry. She was angrier than ever.

"Will you two men do me a favour?" she asked.

Buck looked up. "That's not a fair question, miss. What if I say *yes*. Then you tell me to blow out my brains. First, what do you want?"

"How long you two aim to stay in town?"

Buck looked at Tortilla Joe, who was

studying her over a forkful of *tortilla*. Then he looked back at the girl.

"We don't know for sure," he replied in all honesty. "Lawrence says he won't let us ride out of town. If he kills us I reckon we'll be here a long time. Why do you ask, miss?"

She brushed back more hair. Buck discreetly held his hand over his soup.

"If you stay here," she said, "please eat at some other café."

Tortilla Joe's wide and dark forehead showed a wide and dark scowl.

Buck also frowned. "Why?"

"Those kids. I'll have to wash that front window again soon. I'll lose money on you two, counting my time required to wash the window. Not to mention the cost of the soap."

"Oh," Buck said.

Tortilla Joe had long jowls. "Nobody, not even thees girl, do they want us een thees town of Buckskeen."

The waitress said nothing. She had a frozen, stony face. Buck decided his first impression was and had been

114

wrong. She was not lovely. She was not even pretty. She was, in fact, almost ugly. She looked better walking away than she did walking towards a man.

The door opened. Sheriff Henry Potter waddled in. He said hello to the girl. He nodded at Tortilla Joe who nodded back. He slid his big bottom on to a stool and the stool was absorbed. He looked at Buck.

Buck looked back at him.

"What about the girl?" the sheriff asked.

Buck knew he meant Clair MrCullen. But he decided to act stupid. He scowled and sucked his soup like a carp sucks mud along a Montana creek bank.

"What girl you mean, sheriff?"

"You know who I mean. Clair McCullen."

Buck got to his boots and reached for a toothpick. "What about her?" he wanted to know.

"Why don't you drop charges against her?"

Buck got the toothpick working. "I will," he assured. "But on one condition, sheriff."

The waitress listened. Tortilla Joe reached for a toothpick. The sheriff watched Buck through his red-socketed eyes.

"What's the condition?" Potter asked.

Buck put the toothpick at an angle. "It's this way, Mr. Potter. She thinks she's too wide for her — well, her dress. I'll drop the charge against her if she does one thing — "

"And that?" the sheriff asked.

Buck grinned. "If she kisses me of her own free will, and of her own accord. Otherwise, I press hoss-stealin' charges."

Potter's eyes widened. His wide face got a dazed and pained expression. His voice shook as he asked, "Have you gone loco, McKee? Surely you're joshin' with me?"

Buck kept his face straight. "That's the deal," he said. "And the only deal. You tell her that, sheriff?"

"Sure will."

Buck picked his teeth. Tortilla Joe noisily stuck his toothpick between two teeth and sucked on it.

Sheriff Henry Potter said, "You can't make that horse-stealing charge hold, McKee. You got to remember she took the horse back. No jury in the country would convict her on such evidence."

"Are you a lawyer?" Buck asked pointedly.

"No . . . but . . . "

Just then a man came into the restaurant. He stopped right inside the door. He spoke in a harsh, sonorous voice.

"Stranger, are you Buck McKee?"

Buck went automatically into a crouch. Tortilla Joe moved to one side, hand on his gun. Buck's first impression, coming out of nowhere, was that this man — this human moose — was a Hammerhead gunman Lawrence had hired to match guns with him. He had his hands over his gun.

He glanced at Tortilla Joe. His

117

partner was ready. The Mexican was a hard ball of humanity, crouched and tense. Only Henry Potter seemed unconcerned as he pushed his fork down through a hunk of apple pie.

"Yes, I'm Buck McKee."

The big man wet his lips. He had a tongue the size of a cow's. He stood about six-six, Buck figured. His torso was as thick as the bole of a solid oak. His long arms dangled down to end around his knees.

Buck noticed, then, that he was not ready to draw. Therefore the tension left him, and Tortilla Joe also straightened.

Buck saw a huge face covered with black whiskers. The giant had eyes as big as those of a horse, and they were the colour of a bronc's eyes, too. They were brown and moist.

"What do you want?" Buck repeated. "I'm Buck McKee."

The man boomed out again. His voice sounded like it came from the bottom of an empty wooden barrel.

It rolled across the café and smashed against the wall.

"Friends of Jack Perry, you two?"

Tortilla Joe answered. "We know Jack's papa. Up een Colorado. Now who are you, beeg hombre?"

"Name is Fiddlefoot Garner."

Buck did some hurried remembering. He could place the name nowhere. He glanced at Tortilla Joe.

"I know heem not, Buckshots."

Buck said, "What's about it, Garner?"

Again that booming voice. "I'm boss of the Cinchring Construction Company. Jack Perry owned it, you know. I rode into town to scout things. Also to claim the body of my boss, who was my friend. Some of my skinners are hot under the collar pads about these hellions lynching the boss."

Buck resumed work with his toothpick. "You scared me breathless," he panted. "I figgered you were another Lawrence gunman comin' to notch me off. Set down an' tie into a V of a pie while we talk, Garner?"

They shook hands. He had a grip like a bear's paw, although Buck had never shaken hands with a bear. Then Fiddlefoot Garner sat on a stool. Buck glanced at the floor, half-expecting the man's tremendous weight to push the base of the stool through the flooring. But the flooring held.

"What kind?" the waitress asked.

She pushed back more hair.

"Apple, miss."

"Don't blow me down," the woman said angrily. "I can hear without you hollering, Fiddlefoot."

"Sorry." The giant grinned. Even his ears seemed to move. She slid out a fork. His enormous grizzly paw swallowed it, leaving only the tines sticking out. These went down to smash a hunk out of the pie.

"Jack Perry boasted about you two comin' in, Buck. His dad wrote down that two hell-roarin' gunslingers were on the way down from Colorady."

The fork rose, the piece of pie balanced. The pie hesitated, the big mouth opened, the pie was lost forever.

Juice ran down Garner's jaw. He wiped it away with the back of a hairy hand. "Nice to have two men fast with their guns to side us," he said.

Buck groaned. "We're not gunslingers, fella."

"You shot dead Will March. March was the fastest man on this range, so they said. Thet makes you a gunfighter in my book, McKee."

Buck shook his head.

Tortilla Joe looked very sad. The ease with which Fiddlefoot Garner got outside half a pie — in three bites — seemed to fascinate the Mexican.

Buck said, "Jack had the deal all wrong. We merely were droppin' in on him to give him ol' Sam's greetings. I don't know where the mistake occurred. Either Sam was joshing with his boy, or else Jack was reading something into the letter that wasn't there. We're jes' two little poor drifters, with no kin or even a roof over our heads . . . "

Sheriff Henry Potter, for once, was

smiling. Tortilla Joe also sported a wide grin. Buck was smiling at his own wit. Then he looked at the waitress. She had a glum and gloomy face. No sense of humour, Buck thought. Worst class of woman a man can tie on to.

"Another pie," Garner told the girl.

Buck said nothing. More kids watched. By now the girl did not bother to chase them away.

Fiddlefoot Garner spoke around more pie, blueberry this time. "Well, anyway, Buck, we got a deal for you."

"Yeah?" Buck's tone dripped scepticism.

"Our men wants you to lead us," the construction boss said.

"Lead you where?" Buck asked, playing ignorant.

"Against them Hammerhead devils, of course. We ain't gonna set back an' let Lawrence lynch our boss." Blueberry juice streaked down both sides of his mouth. He reminded Buck of one of those Cocopah squaws who tattoo a line from their mouth's corners each time they get married. "Jack was a damned swell fellow, Buck. Hard worker and a man of vision. He had eyes that saw the day when this desert, with water on it, would bloom like the proverbial rose. Now he sleeps in a restless death, and his soul cries for vengeance."

"You talk een big words," Tortilla Joe said. "You should be writin' the books, no?"

"What was that?"

"I forget what I say, maybe . . . "

Outside a boyish voice was raised in wild roughness. "Read all about it, people. Buck McKee comes to sling a gun for the Cinchring outfit. Tortilla Joe is with him. McKee beats the hell out of Curt Lawrence. Jack Perry's neck is stretched by lynchin'."

The waitress stuck her head out the door. "We want two papers, Pancho."

She gave one to Buck. The tall Texan read the headlines and winced openly. Damn that Sitting Bull Jones! The old editor sure wasn't out to make him, Buck McKee, a bosom friend of Curt Lawrence! Sitting Bull Jones evidently had more courage than he had good sense. Plainly he stood on the side of the Cinchring outfit.

Fiddlefoot Garner boomed, "Sittin' Bull is a brave, brave man, gents."

Sheriff Henry Potter grunted, "A bullet don't care whether it kills a brave man or a coward." This bit of wisdom dispensed, he stood up and paid for his bill.

He speared a toothpick. "Miss McCullen wants to see you, McKee."

"When?"

"Any time."

The obese lawman waddled outside. Fiddlefoot Garner crammed half a pie into his volcanic mouth. He did some talking, and Buck and Tortilla Joe listened. They found out that the Cinchring crew consisted of farmers who had taken up desert homesteads. They had hired a few dirt stiffs — men who knew fresno and slip work. They were going to build a dam and then build some ditches. Irrigation water would flow over the desert. Water that came from Salt River, which had its headwaters high in the mountains.

"Got the dam built yet?" Buck asked.

"Buildin' it now." Fiddlefoot ran a tongue around his plate and looked hungrily at the waitress. "Reckon they ain't no use of me askin' for more pie, is they? Or is my credit good for another half a pie?"

"Ain't no good," the waitress said.

The big man assumed a hurt look. "I figured you was money mad, but I never thought you'd allow a man to starve to death on a stool in your restaurant. Ain't a good advertisement for your café — a man dying of starvation settin' on one of your stools!"

"You won't die of hunger."

The giant eyed the six pies in the case across the counter. "Jes' as you say, woman."

The door barged open. In came Sitting Bull Jones. He chuckled and smiled like he had just inherited a million bucks cash. Buck noticed he had a new ribbon tied around his forehead. This one was blue. There was an acrid odour about the man, not all caused by printer's ink. Sitting Bull Jones could have stood a soaking in Salt River.

He held up his newspaper. "Look at that headline, McKee!"

"My death warrant," Buck said gloomily.

"We got them Hammerhead scissorbills on the run, McKee. When you come in to side us — you two professional gunslingers — "

Buck openly winced.

Tortilla Joe visibly shuddered.

Sitting Bull laid his war club on the counter. "Done drove a spike into it," he said, admiring the club. "Left the head out about an inch. Hey, McKee, where you all headin' for at this time of the evening?"

"Cinchring," Buck said.

The publisher's tan face became pale. His ink-stained fingers grabbed Buck by the shirt sleeve. His fingers were talons twisting the sleeve.

"What about me, McKee?"

"What do you mean?" Buck asked.

"What if the Crown Prince ties into me, when you are gone? I'll be an old, sick man . . . bucking his gun. Consider me, please, Buck!"

Buck had to grin. "What did you do before I arrived?"

"What do you — mean?"

"You bucked Hammerhead then, didn't you? I wasn't around to protect you then."

"But, Buck — Things have come to a head, since then. Since you an' Tortilla Joe came into Buckskin I've shot off my mouth more than ever — I knowed you two gunmen would help me if Lawrence pushed me."

Buck stared down at the wide eyes. He looked at the hairband holding in the greasy hair. A sort of pity came into him.

"What if — Lawrence kills me?"

Buck grinned. "I'll preach your

funeral sermon. Never preached one in my life, but there's a first time for everything . . . so they tell me."

He disengaged the talons. Fiddlefoot Garner swung his gaze back to the pies. The waitress wiped a plate and listened. Tortilla Joe wore a wide, good-natured grin.

"Eef he shoots you bang bang dead, we put the white leely in your hands, Seetin' Bull."

"Hell of a consolation you two buttons are," the old man mourned. "Girl, black coffee — gallons of it, and pronto."

Buck and Tortilla Joe went outside, Fiddlefoot Garner waddling along behind them, mind still on the pie. He had driven a buggy into town. At the hitchrack in front of the General Store he had tied the team of black geldings to the tie-rack. He said he would go out in his buggy. The partners would get their horses from the town livery barn and ride along with him.

"All right," Buck agreed.

8

Crafty Schemers

UNKNOWN to the partners, Curt Lawrence watched them from the bank. He peered out from the corner of the drawnlow blind. Behind him, seated at his desk, was Martin Halloway. Halloway looked at the cowman's wide back and thought, a bullet through the spine would end him for once and for all. He liked that thought.

But this was not the time . . . or the place.

Banker Halloway looked at Sybil Lawrence. She sat on the corner of his desk. She had her legs crossed. Halloway looked at her pretty knees. Suddenly he wanted to put his hand on her knee. The urge was almost irresistible. Still, he choked it.

He had had his hands on her knees before . . .

He looked up at her.

She looked down at him.

Curt Lawrence had his back to them.

He gave her a long and slow look. The look of a lover. She smiled and winked at him. The smile had a brassy and forced edge to it. But Martin Halloway did not notice this. He was too deeply in love.

And love, so some sage once said, wears blinkers.

Curt Lawrence spoke without looking at them. "Fiddlefoot has come in for them, I'll bet. They're heading for the town livery barn. That means they aim to get their broncs. He's turnin' his team and the buggy. They'll head out to Cinchring with him.

"Sittin' Bull Jones is going into his office. Damn him and his *Cactus*. We have to get him outa our way, people."

Again Halloway watched the woman's pretty knees. "A bullet — just one little bullet — in the right part of his

130

anatomy — and in the correct place," he said slowly.

Lawrence added, "And with no witnesses, either."

The banker repeated, "And with no witnesses."

Lawrence straightened. Although it was semi-dark in the office, Halloway could see the rugged set to the man's bony face. Curt Lawrence stood there and thought wrapped him, making him gloomy. His wife watched and swung a pretty leg and said nothing.

Halloway watched, too.

Outside, Pancho called out, selling his newspapers. The words *Lawrence* and *McKee* and *Cinchring* seeped through the brick walls of the bank.

Lawrence said suddenly, "See you later."

Long strides carried him across the room. He went out the back door. Halloway listened to his boots grind down the alley, ringing on the gravel. Back there in that alley a man had died under Buck McKee's hard lead.

Halloway, for some reason, did not like this thought.

He got to his feet. He walked around the desk. He stood in front of Curt Lawrence's wife. They looked at each other. Neither spoke. His hands came down and rested on her knees.

"I love you," he said.

She said, "And I love you."

His eyes searched her face. She slid off the desk and got to her feet. She went into his arms. She pushed against him, emphasizing the correct spots of her anatomy.

They kissed.

The kiss, to the banker, seemed ardent.

"We've got to get rid of him, Sybil," the banker said suddenly.

"We will, Martin."

"When?"

"Now is a good time."

"Why now?"

She said, "McKee and the Mexicans are in town. Already they've had runins with him. Don't you see, Martin?"

He stepped back. He rubbed his jaw and studied her. "Smart little gal," he praised. "Somehow we'd get the blame of his death on McKee and the Mexican. Smart girl, Sybil."

"I have got to own the Hammerhead."

Halloway kept rubbing his chin. His eyes got a crafty and scheming gleam. She had said, *I* have to own the Hammerhead, and she should have said, *We* have to own the Hammerhead. Or was it just a slip of her pretty tongue?

He kissed her again.

Her lips hung to his. Her body hung to his. He stepped back, again deep in his thoughts.

Sometimes she seemed too metallic and too brassy and too scheming. Sometimes it seemed that her mouth pulled down into hard and ugly lines. Sometimes it seemed that her eyes became a little bit too stoney and, at these times, he wondered about her.

But he never wondered long.

He was sure she loved him.

She asked, "Where did Curt go?"

"I don't know," he said.

She said, "I hate the big blowhard devil, Martin. I could kill him myself. He thinks for sure that Jack Perry killed Old John. He thinks for sure that Perry killed his father — "

"Hush, for hell's sake!"

Her smile was touched by cynicism. She cocked her pretty head and regarded him with a long glance.

"The walls don't hear," she pointed out. "Man, are you getting jittery?"

He studied her. "No," he said. He added, "But why take chances?" He walked back and forth, hands behind his back. She watched him but he did not look at her. She was the schemer now, and this showed on her face. But when he looked up the face was smiling and clean.

Halloway stood there with his head cocked. He was thinking of Hammerhead — the biggest ranch in this section of Arizona Territory. The immense ranch-house spread out along the mesa, big and long and made of adobe — the house built by John Lawrence, almost half a century before. And he was thinking of Hammerhead cattle. Cattle, moving ahead of riders during roundup — thousands of cattle, coming out of the mesquite and underbrush, running with wide eyes, smashing through the chamiso and red-shank. They were running across his brain . . . and he wanted them. And he was working his plan, too. Some men went out with a gun or a club, and they got what they wanted — John Lawrence had been that type, and his son was that type, also. They were the kind who tore what they wanted from the earth, from their fellow men. They were tough and domineering, and they walked across the earth in huge strides, the chime of their spur rowels echoing across the rangelands. They took their land and their women and they broke their broncs and they ran out their wild cattle . . . and they fought not with brains, but with brawn.

He was not this type. He knew how to wait, and those men who did not know the meaning of the word *wait*. He was patient, as the spider is patient; he had spun his web, now let the boisterous blowfly get ensnared . . . He would wait and he would scheme, and he would have got what he wanted; if things rushed too fast, and waiting could not attain its goal, only then would he move to meet his adversaries, and his gun would be in his hand.

"A dime for your thoughts, Martin?"

His smile was quiet. "Are you worth a dime, pretty lady?"

"What do you mean?"

"I was thinking of you . . . "

"Oh, quit the joking." She was on the desk again, swinging one pretty leg. She watched him for some time and he had only her face to show her thoughts. And her face showed nothing. He saw her scowl suddenly.

"What's the trouble?" he asked.

"I'm thinking of two men."

"Yes. Could I guess?"

"Go ahead," she said.

He said, "A fat waddling Mexican, and a string-bean cowpuncher. Tortilla Joe and one Buck McKee . . . "

"That's right."

He started pacing again. The thought of the two partners had shoved the pleasing thought of Hammerhead out of his mind. His boots made their sounds — five paces over, five back. He put his hands behind his back.

"We're lucky they came into town," he said suddenly.

"I think so. If we can get one of them to kill Curt."

"I got it figured out," he said.

She nodded. "How will it work out?"

"Fiddlefoot Garner has come into town for them. They'll go out to Cinchring. They'll look the deal over out there. Neither of them are farmers . . . nor do they know a thing about irrigation. But one glance at the fresno-men and they'll be sure of one thing, Sybil."

"And that?"

"That there are no fighters on the outfit. Farmers, yes — and a few drifting dirt-men — but no tough fighters. The farmers are from the east and the midwest; they have been raised in peace. The dirt men are drifters, working only for wages. Am I right?"

"Then what will they do?"

He scowled. He rubbed his gaunt jaw. His eyes showed doubt. "I don't know," he had to admit. "They might move against Hammerhead in open warfare. They might play their cards close. They look stupid and dumb, but McKee killed Will March, and March was no cowpuncher on Hammerhead payroll — Will March was a professional gunman . . . "

"Maybe McKee was lucky?"

Halloway grinned. "Well, he must have had lots of luck since coming to Buckskin, for he's won most of the time." He touched his jaw gingerly. "He knocked me down, for one thing; he laid Curt down, too." Suddenly anger flushed him and his face reddened. "He'll pay for dropping me, woman."

"How?"

He looked at her sharply. "Are you teasing me?"

"No."

Her face was deadpan.

He pulled air into his lungs. "I'll find a way," he assured. "Maybe I can lay the killing on to the shoulders of your beloved husband?"

"Hope so." Again, that pretty leg swung. Again, he watched it. She said, "How about Clair McCullen?"

"What about her?" His voice was sharp.

Sybil Lawrence moved her shoulders lazily. "She's in the calaboose, remember? Horse stealing, the charge — and McKee filed the complaint. Why is he keeping her in jail?"

"He can't hold her."

"She stole his bronc."

He said, "She *borrowed* it, not *stole* it. She took it back. How that damned dumb Potter could have allowed McKee to file a complaint is beyond my understanding. But Potter hasn't got too much between the ears except space."

"You can only push him so far," the woman said. "Then he plants both hoofs and is as bullheaded as a lovesick burro."

"He's small fry. So is Sitting Bull Jones. Two necessary nuisances, one might say. Curt is a fool for taking Sitting Bull so seriously. Wonder where your loving husband went?"

"I wonder . . . "

9

Night Guns

BUCK pulled in his bronc. Tortilla Joe, riding behind him, also stopped his horse.

"What ees the matter, Buckshots? Why you stop your *caballo* at thees place, here een the darkness of thees building?"

"Curt Lawrence . . . " Buck murmured. "Just went in the back door of the saloon. Why don't he use the front?"

"Maybe he come down the alley from the bank, no?"

Buck dismounted, ground-tying his horse. He was the type of man who always played his hunches, and right now he had a hunch something was wrong. He kept remembering the pinched, frightened face of old Sitting Bull Jones. The old publisher had reason for being afraid; that extra about Curt Lawrence would not make the Hammerhead owner a bit happy.

Tortilla Joe also came down out of saddle. He breathed with hoarse sounds, a fat animal on foot. They were hidden in the darkness of the building. Heat still came up from the desert. It hit them in the face, and it was very hot. But neither had any thought for the heat.

"Wonder what he do een saloon?" Tortilla Joe conjectured.

"Come along," Buck said.

They left their mounts and went along the alley. They came to the back window of Thick Neck's saloon. Again, they looked through a window. Curt Lawrence was talking to a man who was playing cards with three other men at a table. The man's back was to them and therefore identification was impossible. Still there was something familiar about the man, Buck reasoned.

"Who's he talkin' to, Tortilla?"

The Mexican looked at the man. "I

no know, Buckshots. Steel, there ees something about him — Now he stand up, no?"

The man had laid down his cards and had cashed in his chips and had got to his boots. Lamplight showed his face clearly. He was the gunman who had held Sybil Lawrence, the one whom she had scratched across the nose. He and Curt Lawrence moved to one side and talked. Lawrence did most of the talking. The gunman merely nodded occasionally. He rubbed his nose gingerly. Then he pulled his gun around and went out on main street.

Lawrence went to the bar. He put his boot on the rail and Thick Neck poured him a drink.

"He ees ask that gonman to do sometheengs for heem," Tortilla Joe said. "I wonder what the task she ees for heem to do, Buckshots?"

Buck frowned. "Let's find out."

Again they went between two buildings and came out on main street. Already Buckskin was retiring. Lamplights were going out in various adobe cabins. The Mexicans got up early, loafed all day, and retired early. No wonder so many dark-skinned Mexican kids ran around, Buck thought wryly. A dog trotted across the street — he was long and lean and wolfish. The store was dark and the only lights in town, on the main street, were those in the saloon, the Greasy Plate Café, and in the *Cactus* office.

Buck pulled at Tortilla Joe's sleeve. "Duck back in this doorway."

The gunman came sauntering along. He did not see them because of the darkness that hid them. He walked by about ten feet away. He was mean and evil and dark, and Buck watched him closely. The gunman sauntered by the *Cactus* office. The press was quiet, the edition had been printed, and the gunman glanced inside. Then, satisfied by what he saw, he walked on. He anchored himself between two buildings. He was a dark, ugly outline against a dark background. Had Buck not seen him enter the slot, he would not have known a man hid there.

Buck said, "I got a hunch Sittin' Bull was right, Tortilla."

"You mean thees gunmans — he ees out after Seetin' Bulls?"

"He looked in the print shop. Sitting Bull wasn't there, of course — he's in the Greasy Plate. The gunman will wait. Nobody on the street. He could grab ol' Sittin' Bull by the hair, drag him into the alley, and club him to death with his gun. And who could prove what?"

"I go een the alley, Buckshots."

Buck nodded. He heard his partner move away. Despite his bulk the Mexican moved on silent boots when he wanted to move in silence. Buck stood in silence and watched. A few minutes ran by. The thought came to the tall Texan that perhaps his assumptions, his hunch, were all wrong. Could be so . . .

Sitting Bull Jones, complete to war club, came out of the Greasy Plate

Café. He turned towards his printing-shop. The moment was ripe and Buck stepped out of hiding. He moved down the street towards the old man. He could well imagine the gunman's surprise upon seeing him on the street. Buck knew that eyes were constantly watching him; the gunman probably figured he, Buck McKee, had gone out to Cinchring Construction. But here he walked the main street, coming towards Sitting Bull Jones.

Sitting Bull Jones, unaware of the killer in the shadows, stopped, stared at Buck McKee.

"Thought you headed for Cinchring, Buck?"

"Gonna get some terbaccer," Buck said. "Found my Durham supply had run out. So postponed it a spell."

"The saloon has Durham."

Buck shook his head. "Don't cotton to the saloon too much. Curt Lawrence is in there and I've had enough hell with him for one day. The girl in the café has tobaccer, hasn't she?"

"Sure."

"S'long, Sittin' Bull."

"So long, McKee."

The old man continued on down the street toward his newspaper office. Buck went towards the café. He was sure the hidden Lawrence gunman had heard every word he and Sitting Bull had said. That was all right. They had told him nothing. Buck didn't need another sack of Bull Durham any more than he needed another head. He had three full sacks in his saddle-bag.

He got opposite the hiding place of the gunman. A cold feeling came in and touched the Texan. He got a queasy feeling in his belly. The gunman could blast out, and he, Buck McKee would get the works. He realized he was going into danger for an old man who, by all rights, should have meant nothing to him. Fate had pulled queer strings. A few hours ago, when he and Tortilla Joe had ridden into Buckskin, neither had even known a queer old galoot like Sitting Bull Jones had even walked the earth.

Now he was moving against a gunman — a Lawrence gunman — because of the old printer.

Suddenly, without warning, Buck pivoted, gun out. He pointed it towards the gunman who imagined he was half hidden.

"Come on out, you two-bit killer."

His words were low and were heard only by the gunman. Sitting Bull Jones, going down the street, did not hear them. Buck could well imagine the gunman's surprise.

Buck cocked his .45. "Come on out, Lawrence man," he said quietly. "I seen you hide yourself back there waitin' for ol' Sittin' Bull. I can see you clear. Take your hand off your gun or I'll send lead howlin' through your brisket."

"Don't shoot, McKee!"

The gunman walked out of hiding. He had both hands discreetly away from his gunbelt. He came close to Buck, staring at his gun.

"You're a hard man . . . to get the best of, McKee."

Buck looked at him. He was no coward. He would fight if he got a chance. Buck egged him on.

"Somebody went through my saddle-bags down at the barn." This was a deliberate lie. Buck had glimpsed Tortilla Joe behind the man. The Mexican was working towards the killer. By the deliberate falsehood Buck hoped to rivet the gunman's attention on him.

"They — did?"

"You were snoopin' around my rig. Somebody told me that. You searched them saddle-bags." Buck stiffened his gun, pointing it at the man's belly. "I should shoot you through the guts and let you die a slow, lingerin' death . . . "

"You can't kill a man without givin' him a chance, McKee!"

"You aimed to kill that old printer. Lawrence went into the saloon and ordered you out here to bump off Sittin' Bull. I saw the whole thing.

149

Did you search my saddle-bags?"

The man's lips trembled, then tightened.

"McKee, you jes' want trouble, that's all."

They were two wolves circling. Fangs bared, manes raised. Ready to fight, to snarl, to bite.

By this time the Mexican was directly behind the gunman. How he moved so quietly Buck could not understand. The gunman had no idea a third man had entered this. He was aware only of Buck.

Buck deliberately holstered his .45. The barrel swished as it went against the oiled holster-leather.

"You givin' me ... a chance, McKee?"

The gunman spoke in a hoarse, rattling tone of voice. His gross body became compact, a human ball of hard flesh, and his hands were down, fingers out over handles of two big .45s.

"I sure am," Buck said.

The gunman watched, eyes glistening

even in the dark. He was evil and mean, and he licked his lips. His tongue was out when Tortilla Joe's club came down. The blow almost made the gunman cut his tongue in two with his teeth. He never knew what had hit him. One minute he had his full senses, his faculties were in co-ordination; he was a fighting tough machine of flesh and blood. The next, he was on the sidewalk, lying on his face — an inert, broken piece of meat and blood, senseless and unaware of the world.

Buck grinned, wiped sweat from his forehead. "I timed it just right at that," he said, and his voice sounded limp. "I thought for a while I had holstered my six-shooter too soon and you wouldn't slug him afore he got to draw. You walk on silent boots, friend."

"I leave my spurs . . . een the alley, Buckshots."

Buck stepped across the unconscious gunman. Not a soul on the street, and nobody to tell the gunman — when he regained consciousness — what had happened. Nobody to report back to Curt Lawrence either. Buck pulled his partner into the pitch darkness between the buildings.

"Come along, Tortilla."

"We leave heem . . . back there?"

"Sure."

"He know not what heet heem. He weel come too and then he weel stagger around — hola, like a drunk mans, no?"

"Lawrence will look for him, I reckon. Where did you get that club, and what is it made of?"

The club was made of manzanita, that tough and flexible red wood of the desert. Tortilla Joe had cut it from a tree back in the alley. He was very cheery and proud of himself, and he continuously chuckled. The Mexican kissed the thin club as loudly as Sitting Bull Jones had smacked his war club.

They came to the alley.

Buck said, "I got another call to make."

"*Si*. Where ees she to be made, Buckshots?"

"The jail."

"Ah, the *muchachita* — the little girl, no? Maybe she kees you now and get out from behin' them col', col' bars, no?"

"Maybe," Buck grunted.

They went in through the front door. From outside the place had looked like it had no lamplight but that was because the blinds completely killed all chance of light showing in the windows. They went in without knocking.

A lamp burned on a wall bracket. It was turned down very low. Sheriff Henry Potter slept in his chair, head on his desk. Lamplight glistened on his greasy bald pate. He was sound asleep. He snored like a jackass braying. His thick lips moved, his big nose quivered; he was deep in the arms of the dark god Sleep. He did not awaken, either, when Buck and Tortilla Joe entered.

"Dead mans," Tortilla Joe joked.

They crossed the office and opened

the door leading to the jail. A lantern hung from the ceiling supplied a dim and inadequate illumination. The jail consisted of six cells, three on each side. A cell corridor ran between them. The partners went down this.

Clair McCullen had been lying on her bunk. When she heard them she sat up and looked around and then she came to the bars.

Buck said, "Even in this dim light, you're sure purty, sweetheart."

"Lovely," Tortilla Joe chimed in.

Her voice was husky. "You come to turn me loose?"

Tortilla Joe shook his dour head. Buck also shook his head. Hope left her face and it turned hard and anger was on her mouth, twisting down her lips.

"McKee, why the hell have you got me in jail?"

"A purty girl — a perfect woman — never swears," Buck chided devilishly. "After all, you have prestige here — you're the town millinery shop — "

"Not *shop*, you idiot! I'm the

seamstress — Oh, Lord, you talk stupid. You talk like I was a store, and I'm only a woman — " She stopped when she saw his smile. "You're getting me mad on purpose."

"And you're fallin' for it," Buck said. He admired her trim and womanly figure, and his grin dripped hunger. "You stole my hoss. Hoss thieves, so they say, have to pay. And you have to pay me, honey."

She tried to slap him through the bars. He grabbed her arm and held it. She tried to pull her arm back but he kept his grip on it. She stopped struggling. Lamplight showed her eyes clearly.

"What is this . . . deal, McKee?"

"You can get out of here on one promise."

She watched him. "If that promise is what I think you mean, then you're out of luck, you long-eared galoot!"

Buck grinned.

Tortilla Joe watched, smile wide.

Silence grew. Buck still held her

arm. He stroked her little hand. He kept on smiling. Finally impatience possessed her.

"What is that . . . promise, McKee?"

"You kiss me, of your own accord — and like you meant it."

She jerked her arm back, the movement savage. "You go and stay put," she snarled. "Why, you — you — "

"Good-bye, honey."

"Don't honey me — You good — You good-for-nothin' — "

Buck broke in with, "You're stuttering. Doesn't look good for a purty girl to get so mad she stutters. Well, when you change your mind, get Potter to come after me. I'm a fool around the women, sister."

"You're a fool — all the time — "

Suddenly Sheriff Potter loomed into sight in the doorway leading to the office. He had a pistol in his hand and his eyes were wild.

"What the hell — ? You scared me silly, McKee. Figgered mebbe it was another jail delivery, I did." He

156

holstered the .45 clumsily, the barrel of the gun first missing the mouth of the holster. "You two walked past me, eh?"

"You sleep hard," Tortilla Joe said.

Buck said, "She won't come across. For one little kiss, she could go. But she's like a mule with the ringbone. Won't move a step, sheriff."

They went into the office. The air was cool but still the sheriff mopped his bald head. Sweat popped out behind his dirty bandana. His huge eyes rolled in their damp sockets. He rubbed his wide nose.

"McKee, do me a favour, please?"

Buck looked at Tortilla Joe. "This deal is kinda got the cart ahead of the hoss, Tortilla. Usually I have to ask the sheriffs for favours. This sheriff is askin' me for one." He spoke now to Potter. "What's troublin' your purty little head, lawman?"

"My wife."

"Never knew you had a wife. What about her?"

Again, that bandana ploughed through sweat. Again, the sweat popped out behind its passage.

"My wife is suspicious of me an' Clair. Claims I'm holdin' the girl to have her close to me — Imagine a man my age — and a woman that suspicious — McKee, drop the charges against her, for me?"

"No."

"My oldest daughter — Aggie — Hell, she won't even talk to me! McKee, she thinks I'm holdin' her because I — "

"You said that before."

They went outside. Down the street Lawrence was kneeling beside his gunman. Buck said, "Let's have some fun."

"This won't be fun," Tortilla Joe said.

"Might be."

The gunman was still out cold. When they approached Lawrence got to his feet. Buck said, "Somethin' wrong, Curt?"

"To you, McKee, the name is

Lawrence — not Curt!"

"Okay, Curt."

Tortilla Joe looked down at the gunman. "Maybe he have his gon go off, an' he keel heemself, no?"

"Somebody's slugged him," Curt Lawrence snarled.

The owner of Hammerhead looked at Buck. His gaze moved over to Tortilla Joe. Buck said, "Too bad, fella."

They went to their horses and rode towards Cinchring.

10

Dusty Skies

EVERYWHERE there was dust. Dust was in the still air, in the coffee, in the hotcakes. It hung across the desert and it coated saguaros and manzanita and sagebrush and greasewood with its grey and gritty coat. It was the tough desert dust of Arizona Territory. Grey dust, fine as silt, tough as sandpaper. Dust rose behind fresnos. It came from under the pounding plodding hoofs of working mules and horses. It rose from under the boots of plodding men. It coated the men's clothing and put a grey blanket across their faces, leaving only their eyes visible. It filled their mouths and the cracks on their lips and they cursed it and they ate it and they slept in it and it filled the pores of their sweaty, stinking bodies.

Men were fighting the desert. Water was on their side, a patient and dumb ally. Men were going to whip the desert. Water would whip it. But first, there had to be dust, and they were fighting the dust so water could be brought in — clear and dashing mountain water — to kill the dust for once . . . and forever.

"Damn this dust," Buck said.

"Damn thees dust," Tortilla Joe said.

Buck looked at the Mexican. "Are you a parrot, too?"

Thick shoulders lifted, fell. "I am accommodatin', senor. You cuss at the dust, I cuss too. You not sleep too well last night, no?"

"Bunk hard as a granite boulder," Buck grumbled. "Pillow filled with lead hunks. Dead men running across my head all night. These hotcakes are a combination of copper filings and sand. You bite into them and the vibrations of your teeth on the grit make your ears wobble and jump."

"Makes my toes ache," the Mexican said.

Buck said, "A man wastes his breath when he talks to you. So keep on chewin' sand, chum, and let this long boy nurse his own bitter thoughts. I wonder how dumb two humans can get?"

"You ees tell me not to talk, remembers?"

"Then why are you talkin' now?"

Again, the Mexican shrugged. Buck would soon get over his angry mood, the fat man knew. Anger never stayed long with his partner. It passed and soon Buck would be joking again. But the dust was thick. Tortilla Joe suspended part of a hotcake in front of his cavernous mouth and sent a glance around the cook-tent. Already the skinners were out moving dirt. The cook was at the far end, peeling spuds for the noon meal. Buck and Tortilla Joe were alone at the long plank table without a table-cloth or oil-cloth. Tortilla Joe shoved the hotcake into his mouth. He chewed on sand.

Buck's teeth grated on sand, too.

But the lanky Texan kept on chewing. A man had to eat to live, was his philosophy. But he didn't give a hoot about this Cinchring dirt-camp. He was a saddle-man — a gent wedded to a horse — But here he was eating a combination sand-and-flour hotcake in a stifling old tent that was once white but now was dark with dust.

"We was born for trouble, Tortilla Joe. Here we are, stuck with a bunch of sodbusters and fresno men building an irrigation system, just because we punched cows for a sick old man up in Colorady. Over on the Gila river awaits the Gallatin spread, and the sun is warm and there's no dust and cattle are grazin' in the foothills, waitin' for us."

"Me, I no talk, remember?"

"Jes' cause we mentioned to Sam Perry we was ridin' across Arizona Territory, he writes to his son — and the cook or somebody makes gunhands out of us. And here we are up to our little dirty necks in gunsmoke."

"I no *habla*, remember."

Buck looked at him. "Say somethin', you fat son of a saddle."

"That Clair, she ees got a purty smile, no?"

"Ain't all she's got that's purty," Buck said.

"Ah, lovely womens, no?"

The Latin sighed gustily. Buck swung his attention over to his partner. He looked at the wide dark face and the thick nose. Tortilla Joe blankly stared back at him.

"Why one look at me, Buckshots?"

Buck grimaced. "That mug of yours would drive a hungry dog off a garbage wagon." He climbed to his tall height and stepped back over the bench. Then he put his knife and fork and spoon on the plate, put his coffee cup around a little finger, and carried the mess over to where the cook's flunky was washing dishes in a copper tub.

"Fine saddle-blankets, cookie."

The fat cook glared at him. "Not *saddle-blankets*, fella. *Hotcakes*," he corrected in a tight voice.

"I still stick by the word *saddle-blankets*," Buck said.

"You're makin' yourself unpopular, McKee."

Buck shrugged. "Makes no never mind."

Tortilla Joe dumped his hardware and plate in the water. "Come on, Buckshots, we go outside, no? The sand ees fresher and tastes better out there, so they is told me a while back."

They walked out. Buck, tall as a toothpick; Tortilla Joe, waddling like a bear. The cook, arms akimbo, glared at them.

"Sure 'ain't grateful," the *cocinero* grumbled.

The flunky, not saying a word, continued washing dishes. Sand continued to sift through the tent.

"Wonder if the wind will come up again today," the cook conjectured.

"Sure hope it don't blow no more sand."

"Don't know," the flunky said shortly. While it had been stifling hot under the tent, outside it was blistering hot. Sunlight hit the sand, reflected, bounced, and gained in heat with each bounce, or so it seemed to Buck. The distant mountains danced in the heat, looking like mirages. Out of the dust and the heat came the huge form of Fiddlefoot Garner.

"Hot," he said.

Buck said, "Hot."

Tortilla Joe said, "*Muy calor*."

These words said, Fiddlefoot Garner wiped his forehead with his hairy hand. He looked at the mountains.

"Nice and cool up there in them pines," he said. "That's where the Salt River comes from. Nice and cool up there."

"Nice and cool," Buck said.

"*Muy cool*," Tortilla Joe said.

Fiddlefoot Garner asked, "Good meal?"

"Sure," Buck said. "Fine grade of sand."

Garner smiled. "You'll get used to it." He ran his forefinger around the inside of his mouth. "Even got it between my teeth. Poor Jack Perry — loved this sand. Hey, wanna see the dam, eh?"

His ox-like eyes went from man to man. Plainly the most important thing to him, in this sand-filled earth, was the dam.

"Why not?" Buck said.

"Si, sure," Tortilla Joe said.

"We'll ride out there," the big man said. "In my buckboard. Come along, I got my team tied over here in the shade."

"Didn't know this country had any shade," Buck said sourly. To himself he said, I don't give a damn about a dam.

Garner had a team of sorrels tied behind the tent. They were dusty sorrels now, and the buckboard to which they were hitched was also dust-rimmed.

Tortilla Joe got in, the buckboard sagging to one side. Garner climbed in on the other side, almost tipping the rig over. With Garner on one side, with Tortilla Joe on the other, the buckboard sort of settled to a levelness. They filled the seat completely.

Buck said, "I'll ride behind the seat, standin' up."

Garner had already untied the team. He cramped the front wheels around, almost tipping the rig over.

"Quite a dam," he said.

Buck nodded.

Garner got the team to a plodding walk. Sand hung to the steel rims of the wheels. Garner said, "Hot day."

Neither partner spoke.

Garner bit off a chew. "You may not know this, McKee, but this mornin' afore you was awake the farmers voted."

"Yeah . . . Voted on what?"

"They voted you in as their leader. They want to avenge Jack's untimely passing. They nominated you and voted

168

you in as gun-boss."

"I ain't got a thing to say about it, eh?"

Garner cocked his head and studied him. "Why, hell, yore an ol' pal of Sam Perry, and Jack is Sam's only son — Think of the honour, McKee."

Buck grinned. "Great honour. What kind of a plan have they hatched up, Garner?"

"Kinda a watchful, waitin' plan, I reckon."

"Good," Buck said.

The team slowed to a stupid plodding. Wind whipped in, dust and sand rose, and Tortilla Joe blew his nose.

"Sand man, that's what I am." he said.

Nobody answered.

Here the desert ran into the brush-covered hills. They went along a trail that led now through cottonwood trees, for the river was close by. They followed a road ground into the hot earth by wheels and hoofs and boots. The dust rolled out of the coulée. It came in billowing, stifling clouds. Plainly they were nearing the dam site, for fresnos raised the dust. Fiddlefoot Garner put the team to the west, and the rig climbed a low hill. Below them were the workers.

Fiddlefoot Garner said, "Down in thet dust is the dam. As you kin see, the river is low at this time of the year; about December it almost disappears. Then the rains fill it again and it runs with more water. Our plan is to get our dam finished afore the winter rains start."

Buck studied the deal. He was amazed at the amount of work the workers had done. They were not disturbing the normal flow of the river. But on each side they had reared their earthen wall. They had the spillway built — a solid sheet of concrete, situated at the west end of the dam. They were lining the face with boulders hauled down from the hills.

Buck said, "When the spillway is completed and the rest of the dam is solid, you aim to run a coffer-dam across the river, eh, an' divert the water through the spillway until you get the old bed of the river covered?"

"That's the deal. And we got to get it built before the rains start, or we lose the hull thing."

Tortilla Joe grunted, "You do lots of work — good work — "

"Jack Perry had his heart and soul — and all his money — in it," the big foreman said. "All of us got our lives' savin's in it, McKee. These farmers has homesteads below here. Most of them are married. Wives stayed back east." He looked toward the south where the desert stretched, saguaros raising ghostly hands against the heat. "This country will all be bloomin' like the Garden of Eden, come a few years. Yes sir, fruit, crops, gardens. Nice homes . . . "

Buck glanced at Tortilla Joe. This big man had a dreamy, faraway look in his horse-like eyes. Up to this point Buck had openly doubted the possibility of turning the desert into farms. Now, seeing the immense work these men had done since spring, that doubt left him. These men would get their goal, come hell or high water . . . or even Curt Lawrence.

Tortilla Joe said, "Good deal, Garner." He nodded his head vigorously. "You make this land good land, I theenk."

"I know it," the foreman said emphatically.

Garner's huge index finger pointed out points — there the main canal would go, angling along the hills, and sidecanals would come off this, running down to homesteads. There would have to be land levelled, a drainage system installed, but they would come with time — the main thing was to get the dam built before the winter rains.

Buck agreed with this.

"You got guards out?" he asked.

"Night and day — twenty-four hours a day — they patrol, Buck. No violence as yet, but we fear Lawrence, when the dam is almost through. It would do him little good to dynamite now, or attempt to destroy the dam."

Tortilla Joe again nodded. "He smart, the hell-son. He wait unteel she ees almost feeneeshed, then he would make hees play."

Buck said, "Don't for one minute underestimate him."

"We ain't."

They spent some more time talking about the dam. Buck began to catch the homestead fever.

Garner asked, boomingly, "You boys ever use your homestead rights?"

"No," Buck said.

"No," Tortilla Joe said.

"We can get you some choice homestead sites." Fiddlefoot Garner was as happy as a boy with a new horned toad. "For you two, anything — "

Buck said, "Not for me."

"Why not?"

"Work," Buck said. "With your hands, too. Not for this boy. I'm so lazy I ride a horse from the corral to the bunkhouse. I wouldn't walk more than a block, unless forced to."

"I only walk half the block," the Mexican said.

Garner's face showed disappointment. "The boys has some nice sites picked out for you two," he reminded. "Think it over. Well, you've seen the dam — now let's drive around the homestead sites, out on the desert."

Buck glanced at Tortilla Joe. The Mexican shook his head. He also didn't relish the idea of bouncing over sand hummocks in a buggy when the thermometer out of the sun stood around one-twenty.

"Can't do it," Buck grunted.

"Why?" Fiddlefoot Garner asked.

"Got to get back to town. Your men are all right out here. We got to get a letter off to old Sam Perry telling him about his son's fate."

"It'll be a hard one to write," Garner said mournfully.

Tortilla Joe nodded. "But we has to do it."

They drove back to the dirt camp. The only shade was that made by the few cottonwood trees along the river bottom. It was so hot that a jackrabbit refused to run. He squatted under a sagebrush, ears back. Garner shot him with his .45, while Tortilla Joe held the lines. But there was no danger of the team trying to run away. Too hot for such gymnastics.

Garner creaked out of the buggy and held up the jackrabbit by the ears. "Chuck for the table," he said. "Figured there wasn't another rabbit around here."

"Why?" Buck asked.

The man creaked back into the buggy, settled his wide bottom on the seat. "We has to live close to our pocketbooks, men. So, rabbits make meals. One boy says he's et so many jacks he's hoppin' around."

Nobody smiled or laughed.

Too hot.

11

The Lonely Land

DESPITE the heat she was still lovely. She leaned forward, arms on the fork of her expensive hand carved saddle. The wind ruffled her silk blouse and showed the fullness of her, and the buckskin riding skirt clung to her full thighs. The polished silver on her hand-made spurs glistened in Arizona sunlight.

"Well," she said, in that throaty voice of hers, "fancy meeting you two here. Tortilla Joe and Buck McKee . . . "

Buck grinned. "I'd take off my hat, Missus Lawrence, but I'm afraid the sun might knock me out of the saddle."

"The same she ees apply to me," Tortilla Joe said, grinning. "I am a polite man, but not when the son ees not polite."

176

Sybil Lawrence's green eyes moved over them. For a moment there was a brief silence. Buck wondered why the wife of Curt Lawrence rode desert range on such a hot day. He watched her face. There was a lot of woman here, and she would show response to the right man . . . He wondered if Curt Lawrence were the right man. From what he had heard, they had been married only a few years. She had come with a show troupe, and she had stayed. Outside of that, and what he knew about her, there was little, if anything, else. She was, he understood, a sort of a mystery. She made no friends, and she plainly wanted none. She liked to drink and she could swear like a trooper, if and when the occasion so demanded . . .

A few head of Hammerhead steers grazed around a hummock of mesquite. To a person not knowing the desert the steers apparently were doomed to starvation. But, strangely, they were fat. They found a little grass around the roots of the mesquite, and they also ate mesquite beans.

"Don't addle your poor little brains," she said almost scornfully. "I take it you two sons of Satan have been out visiting the dirt camp?"

Buck was the spokesman. "That's right, Green eyes."

"Anything new?"

Buck loafed in leather, heat seeping into him. "I had them double the night guard. They're gettin' along fine, they told me."

"And now," she said sweetly, "I suppose you boys are running out of this country, afraid of Curt Lawrence?"

"We got two inquests to go to," Buck pointed out. "One, over Jack Perry; the other, over Will March's carcass. We jes' can't leave, woman."

"No can go," Tortilla Joe said, and shrugged.

She leaned forward even further. Buck saw a ghost of a smile touch her pretty lips. She was all woman and charm. Sunlight reflected from a roll of copper-coloured hair that peeped out from under her cream-coloured Tom Watson Stetson.

"Going to take up homesteads?" she asked.

Buck said, grandiosely, "You're darned tootin', Sybil. Both of us is takin' up a hundred an' sixty, with desert claims to side in, hill claims, mining claims, and the whole works."

"When it get done, we have over a section of land," the Mexican said, falling into line.

She pouted. "Tell that to some fool who believes you, McKee."

"You don't believe us?" Buck said, grinning.

Tortilla Joe assumed a beaten, hangdog look. "All the time nobody she believes us, partner . . ."

Buck said, "We're farmers now, Sybil. Dyed in the wool sod men, we are. Forsaking our hard old saddles for a life of ease. I suppose you are out riding range looking at cattle?"

"If you two classify yourself as cattle,

I'm looking at two bovines, I suppose."

Tortilla Joe mourned, "All the time . . . the eensults, Buckshots."

Buck said, "Stay away from that dirt camp. Those men will figure you're out spyin' for your beloved blowhard husband. They'll jerk your arms out by the roots, and beat you to death with them."

"Oh, gosh."

Buck stretched and swallowed sand. "Well, we got to be on our way to Buckskin, honey. There's a woman in there behind bars and it's drawin' close to the time she'll want to smack me."

"With a board?" she asked.

"Not with a board," Buck said.

She smiled. "Everybody on this range has heard about your crazy proposition, McKee. Do you only play that game with one girl?"

Buck studied her. "You got a husband," he pointed out.

"He's not in the way," she reminded.

Buck put both hands on his saddle-horn and leaned back and looked at

Tortilla Joe, who had a face about as active as a dead lizard in the sun. Tortilla Joe dug a tortilla out of his saddle-bag and unwrapped the corn-husk wrapper with slow determination. His face, Buck saw, was about a thousand years old. Suddenly he winced as his teeth ground on sand.

"Even through the tortilla husk the sand she comes, Buckshots."

Buck said, "One husband should be enough." It was just bantering, conversation. Meaning nothing.

"He is," she said.

"We got to get to town," Buck said.

Tortilla Joe howled suddenly. Both jerked their attention to the Mexican. He had his thumb and forefinger in his mouth.

"I theenk maybe I breaks the tooth, Buck."

Buck grinned.

Sybil scowled.

Tortilla Joe said, "And the Big Fella, he keeck two tooths out of poor Weel

March . . . Waste of tooths, that ees." He stared at his thumb as though he expected to find a tooth impaled on it. "I could use them two tooths."

"Who couldn't?" Buck asked.

Tortilla Joe looked at Sybil Lawrence. "There ees the dentist ees there not een Buckskin?"

"Blacksmith pulls teeth."

"No," Tortilla Joe said suddenly. "I no see heem . . . Already my tooth she ees better."

Buck looked at Sybil. "Ever do any rasslin'?" he asked innocently.

She studied him as though doubting his sanity. "Wrestling? What do you mean, McKee?"

"With the boys," Buck said. "Don't you like to have their tender arms around your little waist — "

"You two," she said convincingly, "are loco."

This knowledge dispensed, she turned her horse sharply, used her spurs and, despite the heat, loped away. Buck watched her and grinned. Tortilla Joe watched and said, "My tooth she ees no break. That was the what you call eet — the act, no?"

"She got mad," Buck said.

Soon mesquite and manzanita hid the wife of Curt Lawrence. The partners jogged along, suffering under the sun.

"Why for she ride range thees hot weather, Buckshots?"

"I dunno," Buck had to admit. "Maybe out spyin' for her ol' man, eh? But still, she cain't love the big stiff."

"Not when she ees kees that good-lookin' banker."

They rode at a walk. Neither was in a hurry. Buck gave Curt Lawrence some thought. When irrigation came in, free range went out. Hammerhead cattle ran over free range, government grass. With irrigation water flowing through canals, more farmers would come — Hammerhead would go broke. For the success of Hammerhead ranch, in this range of marginal land, depended upon free grass. They rode about a mile and then Tortilla Joe said, "Rider he ees come."

The rider turned out to be Curt Lawrence astraddle a bay stallion. A heavy, tough animal, this stallion, and his hard ride had brought sweat out on him. Buck wondered if the big man were out to kill the bronc by riding him so hard in this terrible heat.

The partners drew rein and waited. Lawrence curbed the stud around. The magnificent bay reared against the cruel indignities of the spade-bit. Lawrence hit him with his quirt and forced down his head, and hoofs.

"You two gents seen anything of my wife?" he demanded.

Buck shook his head, face very stupid. Lawrence looked at Tortilla Joe, who looked like he had just lost his entire family.

"We no see her, beeg man."

Buck said, "Only human we've seen since leavin' Cinchring has been you, Lawrence. And man alive, are we glad to see you!"

The heavy face scowled. "Don't get sarcastic, McKee. I don't cotton to your tone of voice, fella."

"Send another gunman against me, then," Buck taunted. "Get another boy along the cut of Will March, and send him against me, eh?"

"There's plenty of time, McKee."

"That's good," Buck said. "So long, Lawrence."

"Maybe I ain't leavin'?"

Buck shrugged. "We don't want you," he said evenly.

They looked at each other. Lawrence ran his fingers slowly over the gold piece in his chin-strap. His hand left the nugget and settled on the fork of his saddle ahead of his .45.

Lawrence remembered things. The body of a man, hanging on a rope, turning slowly in the slow wind . . . Buck slapping a twenty-dollar gold piece from his hand to the ground . . . Yes, and the hard knuckles of Buck McKee knocking him, Curt Lawrence, to the floor . . .

Hate filled him.

Buck saw this hate ebb into the man's face, tighten the thick cords in his thick neck. For a moment he figured the owner of Hammerhead might make his draw. Buck stiffened, fingers moving slightly as he flexed them. His eyes were riveted on Lawrence.

Then, Lawrence remembered Tortilla Joe.

He sent a hard glance toward the silent Mexican. Tortilla Joe was tight in leather, dark eyes bright and sharp.

"Two against one, and odds no smart man would take," Lawrence grumbled.

"Maybe you're not smart," Buck reminded.

Lawrence turned the stallion, cakewalking him around on his hind legs. His grip was savage and hard on the reins. His spurs hit the stud, straightened him, and he loped into the brush. He rode south.

Tortilla Joe said, "He go south. Hees *espousa* she go north."

186

"His back ain't as purty as hers," Buck said.

Tortilla Joe spared enough moisture to spit on a lizard on a rock. "She ees een love with the banker."

"How do you know it isn't a pose — a fake? Maybe the banker has something she wants."

"No fake. Her eyes, they light up — kerosene lamps, they behind her eyes. Love, they say, ees the great theeng."

Buck did not dispute that. Each man, he figured, had a right to his own opinion, as long as he did not try to force his opinion on others . . . For some reason he kept thinking of Banker Martin Halloway. He was a slick customer. Buck sighed and mopped his forehead and restored his stetson to position. Where did the banker tie into this, and what was his game . . . if any?

"Maybe we should rob a bank, Tortilla Joe."

Tortilla Joe sighed. "Eef they catches

us . . . eento the jail we goes. We no need *dinero*, Buckshots. We steel got some of our summer wages. We got the jobs waitin' for us in Yuma weeth Gallatin . . . eef ever we gets to the Gila. I no want to go to jail."

"They'd have to catch us," Buck said.

"Si, but lately the luck we have ees all bad." The Latin sighed again, gusty and loud. "What bank does we rob?"

"Halloway's bank."

"We theenk eet over, no? Thees Seebil, now. Maybe she be married before she marry Lawrence, no?"

"Why ask?"

"Jes' wonder, Buckshots."

Buck gave this consideration. "Sybil is the type what can't sleep alone," he finally said. "So you can reckon she was married afore she met Lawrence. Wonder how long this banker has been on this range?"

"I no know."

They jogged along, nursing silence and their thoughts. A road-runner, weary from travelling ahead of their horses, stopped and rested, wings out to let air get to his wiry body. He stood with his beak open and watched them ride by, secure in the shade of a mesquite clump.

Tortilla Joe looked at the ungainly bird. "Weeth hees beak he can cut the rattlesnakes een two. Hees beak she ees sharp as the teensnips, no?"

Buck nodded. He glanced at six head of Hammerhead cattle out in the brush. They were crosses between Herefords and *cimarrones*, the native Arizona cattle. They were working towards a spring in a draw. Their habit, Buck knew, was to drink in the morning, spend that day working away from the water-hole spring, then work back the next day, spending a night around a water-hole.

"They no graze much off the soil," Tortilla Joe said. "They browse like the deer — hola, there ees one streepin' mesquite beans off the trees, no?"

"Yes," Buck said wearily.

Suddenly Tortilla Joe pulled in his mouth. His stubby and brown forefinger pointed to a rimrock ledge ahead on the side of a butte.

"There ees a rider on thet butte. I see the sun reflect from something shiny, Buck."

Buck reached back and unbuckled his field glasses. He put them on the rider, who was about four miles away. He could not identify the man. He handed the glasses to his partner.

Tortilla Joe focused the adjusting-screw.

"That ees the banker, Buckshots."

"You sure?"

"Sure, Halloways, eet ees."

Buck put the glasses back in the case. When it came to eyes and ears, Tortilla Joe was a human wolf. He always blamed his good eyesight on the fact he had never learned to read and write.

"Why for he ride up there on thet heel?"

Buck said, "He's ridin' so he should meet Sybil, ain't he?"

"They both ride straight, they meet."

"Oh," Buck said.

"Love," Tortilla Joe chortled.

About a mile out of Buckskin, another rider came towards them. He rode with such mad haste that Buck said, "The devil must be goosin' him with a red-hot iron, eh?"

"Maybe he try to keel his horse?"

The rider came closer and turned out to be none other than Sitting Bull Jones. He crouched on the horse like a miniature ape. When he saw the partners he reined in with sand shooting upward. He still toted his war club, Buck noticed.

His face, streaked with sweat, was wild and unruly.

"Clair McCullen — She busted jail, men — "

Buck had to smile. "What's so bad about that, Sittin' Bull? What I'm interested in is this: how did she do it?"

"The sheriff — Potter — He ran off with Clair!"

This news made Buck stare. Tortilla Joe's eyes showed surprise. Buck shut his mouth and studied the man. Was he crazy?

"That the truth, Sitting Bull?"

"They run off together, McKee."

Buck had to laugh. He got a sudden mental vision of Sheriff Henry Potter. Big as a moose, slow-moving as a glacier, and as ugly as a skinned skunk. He thought of Clair McCullen and her cool, blonde beauty. When it came to making perfect pairs somebody has sure mismatched these two.

"Well, I'll be damned," Buck said.

"That purty girl," Sitting Bull said. "And that homely, ugly man . . . Buck, be careful, when you ride into town."

"Why?"

"Mrs. Potter's got a shotgun and says she'll shoot you on sight!"

Buck scowled. "I never even have met this woman. Why does she crave to shoot a hole through me?"

"She blames it all on you. You had Clair tossed into jail, remember?"

Buck looked mournfully at Tortilla Joe. "First thing you know, Tortilla, they'll blame this heat on me . . . "

"Always the trouble," the Mexican said mournfully.

12

Gunsmoke!

HANDS behind his head, Buck McKee lay on his back and admired the ceiling, which had apparently recently been painted an egg-shell blue. The bed he lay on was soft, the mattress good, and the blue silk spread had not been rolled off. But Buck was considerate; he had taken off his boots.

Beside him lay Tortilla Joe who already was dozing off. Buck studied the egg-shell blue ceiling and gave vent to some deep philosophy.

"Now why would a woman who is unmarried want a big double bed like this one we are flopped on, Tortilla Joe?"

"Maybe she gets married once in a while." Tortilla Joe spoke with a large yawn. "First time I've been on a clean bed since the time we stayed in the hotel in Great Falls, up in Montana. Hola, we were the beeg ones that time, no — moneys in all pockets, an' ready to head south for the wenter."

"That was five years ago," Buck said.

"That long . . . already?"

Buck said, "That's gone past. This sure is a nice mattress. A woman sure can keep a room clean, compared to the way a bachelor keeps his quarters. Sometimes I think marriage is worth puttin' up with a woman . . . "

"What eef you marry one who keeps the dirty house?"

Buck grinned. "I'm jes' talkin to hear my big mouth say words, I reckon. If you — even you — was a woman . . . I'd never marry you."

"Thanks for the compleement."

Tortilla Joe started softly snoring. He could go to sleep instantly anywhere at any time. Buck looked at the walls. They too had recently been painted, and their colour was light green. When he had been in grammar school years before one of the teachers had told him the world was green because green was easy on the eyes.

A heavy, thick rug covered the floor. The edges of the floor, showing around the outside of the rug, were slick and clean. Against the one wall stood a mahogany dressing-table with a big mirror. There were two matching chairs, a big cedar chest, and a wardrobe trunk. The door to the clothes closet was open. Dresses hung from the rod — blue, yellow, all colours.

The air had a slight trace of perfume. Buck wrinkled his nose and sniffed. He liked that perfume.

"Evening in Buckskin," he said.

Tortilla Joe slept sounder, and his snores increased in volume. Buck poked him in the ribs with his elbow and the snoring stopped momentarily. Outside, feet approached, and Buck heard them scuffle the sand. He listened closely.

"Sitting Bull Jones," he said. "I can tell the sound of moccasins."

Tortilla Joe came awake. "What was that?"

"Close your mouth," Buck said.

The moccasins scraped sand, came to the closed door, then stopped. There was a short pause and the partners listened and were silent. Then, there came a knock on the door.

Buck said sweetly, "Come in, honey."

He made his voice sound feminine.

The door opened. Sitting Bull Jones, complete even to war club, slipped inside. He closed the door behind him. Then he stood there, back to the door, blinking his eyes. His homely face showed anger and surprise.

He stared at them.

"Buck an' Tortilla Joe, layin' on thet bed! Where is the woman?"

"What woman?" Buck asked.

"The one what invited me in jes' a minute ago?"

Tortilla Joe smiled widely. Again Buck made his voice sound like that of a woman. He said, "Hello, Sitting Bull."

The publisher's ugly face turned very red. He swung his war club in a circle, narrowly missing a chair.

"Damned female impersonator," he roared. "I wondered why Clair would call me such names . . . I never was very friendly with her. Not my fault, though. Did my best to get chummy with her, I did."

"So did I," Buck admitted.

The eyes probed them. "What you two sheepherders doin' in her room, floppin' on her bunk?"

"Waitin'," Buck said.

"Fer what?"

Buck spoke to Tortilla Joe. "What are we waitin' for, *amigo*?"

"We wait for reduction in the taxes, no?"

"No," Buck said. He looked at Sitting Bull. "How come you come up to Clair's home?"

"Jes' wanted to look around. Don't seem possible a purty girl like her would run off with a walkin' garbage pail like Potter. Older than her by years, an' ugly as sin with its paint washed off."

"You're no beauty winner," Tortilla Joe said.

"I know that." Without being offered an invitation, the editor sat down on a chair. He looked at his war club. "Done polished the head of that spike. Now when I swing it, sunshine reflects off it. Tells me instantly whether the spike is on the upper or bottom, so I can hit right with it. Wonder what happened to thet Lawrence gunman last night?"

"Which one?" Buck asked.

"The one thet they found cold on the sidewalk. You fellas talked to Lawrence about him. Found him right after I said good night to you, remember."

"Wonder what happened to him?" Buck asked.

"Maybe he get seeck and fall down," Tortilla Joe said.

"Hawkins don't know what happened

to him either," the publisher said. "He says the first thing he knew he was out cold. Somebody said he'd got a big welt acrost his skull."

"Prob'ly fainted," Buck said. "Hit somethin' with his head as he fell."

Tortilla Joe closed his eyes. Buck looked at the egg-shell blue ceiling. Sitting Bull spat on the head of the spike driven in his war club. He got some fine sandpaper from his pocket. He started polishing the head of the spike.

Buck asked, "How come you're here, Sittin' Bull?"

"Thought maybe Clair McCullen would sneak back for her clothes. Don't seem natural she'd leave with the sheriff, to start with, and it looks like she done left all her clothes behind, too. Thought mebbe I could waylay her and get an interview for the Cactus from her."

"An exclusive interview," Buck said.

"Yeah, exclusive . . . I still don't believe she fell in love with Potter.

His bald head is too shiny and his belly too big.

A fat man — especially one what's bald — he ain't a romantic figure."

Neither partner answered.

Sitting Bull adjusted the ribbon around his head. This time he had a wide green ribbon holding down his hair. He then resumed polishing the head of the spike.

Finally Buck asked, "How long you bin in Buckskin, Sittin' Bull?"

"About four years." Sitting Bull breathed on the spike, polished it some more. "Never selected the town. It chose me."

"How come that?" Buckskin asked.

"I run out of . . . funds. The stagedriver done booted me off the stage. Ol'boy here was runnin' a lousy lookin' sheet. I went to work for him. He wanted to go to Californy. He done gave me the whole caboodle. I couldn't let him do that so I borrowed a few bucks from the bank and gave it to him as a partin' gift. I still remember them tears in his eyes and how his old adam's apple bobbed up and down in gratitude."

"Borrowed the money from Martin Halloway, eh?" Buck asked.

"Not from Halloway 'cause he wasn't the banker at that time. Old Man Jessups owned the bank then. He sold out to Halloway about two years ago . . . yep, two years gone this very month, men."

"Where did Halloway come from?" Buck wanted to know.

"He read ol' Jessups' ad in the Tucson paper."

Buck again devoted his attention to the ceiling. His mind was full of ideas. They were groping around and now they were beginning to arrange themselves into a somewhat orderly fashion. The information given him by Sitting Bull Jones was being woven into this scheme.

Deliberately he changed the subject. "Thet Mrs. Lawrence shore's got an hour-glass figure. Sure would like to get my long arms around her pretty little waist, Sitting Bull."

Sitting Bull Jones' eyes had glistening lights darting across them. He grinned lopsidedly and rubbed his nose.

"I've done been pestered by the same idea many a time, Buck. The big shot sure got dumped off his bronc when he saw her. First thing a man knew, they was man an' wife."

"That quick, eh?"

"That quick," the publisher reported. He squinted at the nail in his club. "Looks darned good to me."

Again, the ideas started moving across Buck's brain. He wasn't the smartest man in the world, and he would have been the first to admit this fact — still, as he often said, he was smart enough to feel hungry, be cold, and feel heat. His mind went to work.

He added up all the things he had learned while in Buckskin. Into this mess he threw the memory of the occurrences that had hit him and

Tortilla Joe in the last few days. It was quite a mess of porridge. He threw one fact against the other, and he got exactly where previous thinking-bouts had taken him — up against a blank wall of ignorance.

"So long, Sittin' Bull," he said.

"I ain't leavin' yet."

"Oh, yes, you are." Buck spoke with emphasis. "My partner and I crave some sleep. Goo'-bye."

Sitting Bull Jones got to his moccasins. He made a sweeping swing with the war club. The nailhead whistled slightly. He juggled the club and smiled. He was as happy as a porcupine who had just discovered a field of tender young corn stalks.

"Sure got the right heft and feel now," he said happily. "I'd sure like to hit Lawrence acrost the rump with it, nail out."

Buck said, "When you hit him, hit him acrost the head — not the rump. For the last time, so long."

Sitting Bull shouldered his war club.

"You're an o'nery ol' woman," he said sarcastically. "So long."

He left.

Buck listened to the crunch of the old man's retreating moccasins. He tried to swing his thoughts into line again but they were stubborn. Tortilla Joe lay on his back with his mouth wide open and his nose vibrating with snores. Buck went to sleep before he knew it. When he awakened he came awake suddenly. His first impression was that he had slept for some time for the shadows of sundown were in the room. He glanced at the door.

It was slowly opening.

He had hold of his .45, and as he identified the figure, he slid the gun back under the pillow. He realized that Tortilla Joe had quit snoring. Evidently the Mexican had awakened even before he, Buck McKee, had come awake. The person who had entered had not as yet seen them lying on the bed because the shadows were thicker on this side of the room.

Buck said, "Why, hello there, honey!"

The figure stopped, became frozen. Buck thought, a lovely little bit of frozen girl, that woman. The woman had her back to them, for she had been going toward the clothes closet. She stood like that — stiff, awkward, unyielding. Then she turned around and peered at them.

"Who the hell are you?"

Buck said, "Shadows almost hide us, eh. This is Tortilla Joe an' Buck McKee, Clair."

Tortilla Joe said, "You come back to veeseet us, no?"

"No," she said stiffly. The shock seemed to have left her now. Buck saw her pretty outline and he wished it were lighter, for he could not clearly see her face. He sat on the edge of the bed.

"Sit down, Clair," he said.

Stiffly, she sat on the chair that Sitting Bull Jones had sat on while polishing the spike in his war club.

Her voice was strained and little high

of pitch. "What the hell are you two devils doing in my home . . . and on my bed?"

Buck grinned. "We come in to take a nap."

"You elopes weeth the lawmans," Tortilla Joe explained. "Your beeg bed, shee ees the empty. We come een an' take the shuteyes, no . . . "

"I'll holler . . . holler."

Buck's smile widened. "Open your purty mouth to scream, kid, and back into the clink you go pronto. This town is as fidgety as a bull what has been high-lifed and turpentined for the ring. One beller outa you an' citizens will descend like hailstones on a wheat-field."

She bit her lip.

"Well," she asked, "What do you want?"

Buck watched her. "Where is Sheriff Henry Potter?"

"I don't — know."

Buck shook his head. "I've never called no woman a liar afore, Miss

Clair. You never busted jail, sister. Potter let you out . . . and he had a reason for turnin' you loose."

"Smart gink, eh?"

Buck was modest. "I'm not too damn' wool-blinded to see my long nose," he assured. "Potter wanted you out of jail for a reason. And that reason wasn't to ride out alone and entertain you in the badlands."

"You're wrong there, McKee."

"Talk," Buck said.

Tortilla Joe sat on the bed, a human ape in the dusk. Buck watched the girl closely. The thought came that he should frisk her for possible weapons. She did not look too calm. She looked jittery and tired and raw-nerved.

"He got me out in the hills, Buck. Then he tried to force himself on me. Get that, Buck! That big stupid fat oaf — he tried to get the best of me."

Buck had a mental picture of that.

"What happened?" he asked.

"I busted him with a left hook. My knuckles still ache. I hit him right in that fat mug of his. And you know what?"

"What?" Tortilla Joe asked.

"I knocked him down. Believe it or not, a little thing like me — and him as big as a steer — and I knocked him flat."

Buck said, "Hard hitter, eh? Where is Potter now, Clair?"

"Said he was going to leave the country for good. He's had lots of pressure on him lately. His wife and kids jaw at him night and day, night and day. Then he lost Jack Perry to the mob — "

Buck shook his head. "He never *lost* Perry," he corrected. "He *gave* him to Lawrence's mob."

"You're plumb wrong there, McKee."

"In what way?" Buck asked.

She shook her head slowly. "Potter was knocked cold; it was a genuine jail delivery. Somebody slugged him cold, hitting him at the base of the skull. The blow landed low — that's why you two never saw it — Potter is honest, men."

Buck grimaced. "There goes a pet theory of mine all up in smoke," he told Tortilla Joe.

"Maybe thees girl — she not honest?"

"Don't call me a liar, you Mexican?" Clair was ready to fight again. Evidently her fistic victory over Potter, out in the badlands, had only whetted her appetite for further fisticuffs.

"I takes eet back," Tortilla Joe said hurriedly.

Buck had another set of questions. "All right, Clair, look at it this way. We'll admit then that Potter maybe is honest. Then why doesn't he head back for town — why is he out in the hills?"

"You got me — stumped, Buck."

Buck eyed her steadily. "Potter has told you secrets, sister. You're anything but a nice quiet little seamstress, believe you me. Might Potter be out ridin' range an' layin' low for a spell while he scouts Hammerhead cattle?"

"I don't know."

Buck glanced at Tortilla Joe. The

Mexican watched Clair McCullen. Buck sensed that the time had come, that the clock showed the right hour.

"Potter might be wise to something," Buck added, speaking in a slow voice. "Did he ever mention to you that the Hammerhead outfit was losin' cattle, Clair? He ever say that?"

"Yes," she admitted, "he did."

Buck was adamant. "What else did he tell you, honey?"

She was silent for a while. Another cur barked across town, and children hollered as they played tag. These sounds seeped into the room.

Buck said, "You and Potter have been good friends. Don't ask me how I know . . . I just know." He was shooting a lot of ammunition into the dark. He hoped an occasional bullet would hit close to the mark, if not on it. He was playing every angle he knew. "Why did he take you out of jail?"

"To get me out in the hills. He admitted that, himself. When he saw

211

he couldn't get to first base, he changed his mind."

"Why is he staying in the hills?" Buck's tone had risen a little.

She moved in the chair, eyes on him. "All right, McKee, I'll tell you what I know. He's afraid they might kill him."

Buck wet his lips. "Who might kill him?" he asked.

"Curt Lawrence . . . or some Hammerhead killer. This has come to a show-down, Buck. You and Tortilla Joe have brought it to a head. According to Potter, Lawrence has to make a move, and do it fast. And he's afraid Lawrence might kill him."

Buck shook his head.

"You don't — believe me?" she asked.

"Not Lawrence. Lawrence won't kill him." Buck shot another question at her. "Sister, where do you fit into this dirty deal?"

Her eyes were on him. He thought,

wish the room was lighter, so I could see her face more clearly. The bed springs moved behind him as Tortilla Joe shifted positions. But Buck had no eyes for his fat partner. His gaze was on the woman who apparently was silently considering his question.

"Talk," Buck said.

She said nothing.

Buck said, "This is goin' end soon. It might end in court and it might end in gunsmoke. I got an answer figured out to this deal. You claim you loved Jack Perry. Lawrence had him lynched. Therefore you must hate Lawrence. We can get Lawrence, but first you have to tell us all your troubles."

She said, "Yes, I loved Jack. Loved him with all my heart — I wanted to marry him — we had planned our home. I'll do all in my power to get even with Curt Lawrence, Buck."

She started to weep. Almost silently she wept. Buck felt his throat tighten, and he looked at Tortilla Joe, who had a mute animal look across his wide jowls. Suddenly Tortilla Joe stiffened. Buck had also heard the noise.

From out in the alley came the sounds of a violent scuffle. Men grunted, and gravel moved under boots. Buck leaped to the door with his .45 drawn. Tortilla Joe was behind him, pistol also palmed.

Clair McCullen watched, sniffling a trifle.

She did not go to the door. She saw surprise run across Tortilla Joe's face. She saw a smile twist Buck McKee's lips.

"Come on in, Sittin' Bull," Buck said.

"That I'll do, Buckshot."

Sitting Bull Jones entered. He dragged a man behind him. He had the man by the legs and the man was out cold. Buck grinned when he recognized the unconscious man. Tortilla Joe said nothing.

Clair McCullen said, "That's the Lawrence gunman, Hawkins!"

13

Trail to Trouble

BLOOD dripped down the man's face from his scalp. He needed a shave and his face was skinned, for Sitting Bull Jones had dragged him face down through the sand and gravel.

Buck looked at Tortilla Joe. "That's the button you knocked out last night with that manzanita club, Tortilla?"

"Thet is the same mans, Buckshots."

Sitting Bull Jones cackled like a hen who had laid a striped egg. "Figgered you gents had laid him low last night . . . And here you lied to me with such straight faces, too. You two are clever gents, believe you me . . . "

Buck asked, "How come you slug him?"

"Glimpse him snoopin' around, Buck.

Gave him the war club, spike and all. Gotta drive that spike in a mite further, though. Cut his scalp too deep, an' I only deliver the coup-de-grace with a glancing blow along the top of his dumb skull. Wonder if I kilt him?"

He felt the man's dirty wrist.

"He's alive," he said.

Buck asked, "How come you was snoopin' aroun', Sittin' Bull?"

"Come down to check to see if Clair had snuck in." He looked at the seamstress. "Glad to see you back, girlie."

"I'm not glad to see you."

"That should hold you, Sittin' Bull," Buck grinned and spoke to Tortilla Joe. "This guy stinks. He belongs in the nearest garbage barrel, Tortilla."

"You grab hees boots, Buckshots. I take heem by the arms, no. We totes heem down the alley until we find a barrel, hola!"

Buck got the unconscious man by the boots. Tortilla Joe got hold of the man's arms. They toted the gunman outside.

Buck had to smile — this was the second time within hours that Hawkins had been knocked unconscious. They found a barrel and they doubled the man and sat him in it. His head hung on one side of the rim and his boots stuck out on the other side.

Hawkins kept on sleeping.

Tortilla Joe rubbed his hands together, studied the unconscious gunman, and then smiled widely.

"Weesh Lawrence could see heem now," he chortled.

Buck said, "We should be riding out of this jerkwater burg soon. I got a hunch this thing will all be over inside a few hours, Tortilla Joe."

"Young Jack — he then sleep in pieces."

"*Peace*," Buck corrected. "Not *pieces*."

"The cart I always get before the horse," Tortilla Joe lamented. "Bet thet Seetin' Bull, he get his interview now, no?"

They returned to the room. Sitting

217

Bull had not got his interview yet. But he had got slapped across the mouth. He was rubbing his jaw when the partners entered.

"Try to kiss her?" Buck asked.

"My youthful ardour overcame my mature logic," the printer said. "She hits as hard as a young burro kicks."

"One jackass hittin' the other," Buck said. He spoke to Clair. "Give the ol' boy a private interview, honey."

"That's all I will give him," the woman said.

Buck and Tortilla Joe resumed their seats on the bed. Clair and Sitting Bull talked with Sitting Bull taking notes in shorthand. Buck noticed the girl told the publisher an entirely different story than she had told him and Tortilla Joe. She was lying to Sitting Bull. Or, had she been lying to them, and telling the truth to Sitting Bull Jones?

Buck decided she was an accomplished liar. She had had much practice, he realized, in the deceptive scheme of fabrication. Sitting Bull Jones concluded his interview, rubbed his jaw, and looked at Buck.

"Gotta git this into print right pronto."

"When will it come out?"

"An extra, as soon as we can grind it out."

Buck said, "Make tracks."

Sitting Bull scurried outside. They heard his moccasins scamper down the gravel and go beyond the range of sound. Tortilla Joe stretched and yawned lavishly.

"I am the sleepy boy," he told Buck.

Buck yawned, too. "Well, let's hit the hay, Tortilla. Got this clean, wide bed — What's the matter with you, woman?"

"You two get out of my bed! I'm sleepy myself — had no sleep last night — "

Buck said, "This bed is wide enough for three."

"I won't sleep with you two drifters!"

Buck lay down and smiled at the

egg-shell blue ceiling. "There's always safety in numbers, honey."

Fully dressed except for their boots, he and Tortilla Joe dozed off. Clair still sat in the chair. Right before sleep took him Buck heard her move over and bolt the door.

She went to bed between them. She shivered. She whispered, "Buck, are you awake?"

"Yes . . ."

"I'm cold. Put your arm around me."

Buck pulled her close to him. He liked the perfume of her hair and the feel of her curvaceous body against him.

"You're not cold," he said.

"I am too." She shivered again.

Buck pulled her closer. Suddenly she began to weep silently. Buck felt her shoulders shake.

"I miss Jack . . . so much."

"Go to sleep, honey."

She was still weeping quietly when he dozed off. He kept his arm around her.

Tortilla Joe slept like he was a dead man. Buck awakened at dawn and they were both still asleep. Tortilla Joe also had an arm around Clair. She slept soundly, mouth opened slightly. Buck looked at her pretty face with the dawn colouring it. She was a beauty. Her hair was tumbled across his shoulder, and her breathing was deep and secure.

He looked at Tortilla Joe.

The Mexican slept with his mouth opened. He breathed out a violent mixture of odours associated with onions and garlic and beans.

Buck said, "My God, he's homely."

Clair moved and opened her eyes. She looked at him and smiled. Buck had been groping for a decision, and now he apparently reached it.

"Tonight we got a job to do, Clair."

"All of us?" she asked quietly.

Buck nodded.

"What is it, Buck?"

"Tonight we rob a bank," Buck said.

14

Rimrock Rendezvous

SHERIFF POTTER ate like a wolf who hadn't seen a jackrabbit for two weeks. He crammed the sandwiches into his wide mouth. He spoke around half a sandwich, and his words were muffled. He kept on chewing and talking.

"I had to get out of town, McKee. They had the pressure on me plumb hard. Hell, I was afraid they might shoot me down!"

Buck sat cross-legged in the shade of a granite boulder. "Then thet jail delivery was the real thing, eh?"

Potter bit deep into a ham sandwich. "Good chuck, fellas." His head bobbed in the positive. Sun glistened on his bald dome like it was made of polished silver. "Thet was the real thing," he said.

Buck looked at Tortilla Joe, who sat opposite him. He sat cross-legged and he was humped over like a bullfrog sitting on a log.

"What strikes me as odd," Buck said slowly, "was that you never recognized a one of the lynchers . . . "

"They all wore masks and raincoats and old overcoats — anything to hide their identities . . . Two of them come into my office with them Jesse James disguises and *blotto* — this lawman is out cold."

Buck nodded.

"Talk more maybe?" Tortilla Joe asked.

Clair McCullen, leaning against the boulder, also in the shade, watched and listened carefully, but kept out of the conversation. The whole thing was tying itself into a compact part now, Buck realized, and he was getting rid of the loose ends, doubling them back and making them take on meaning.

"Lawrence has to get Cinchring out of this country," the lawman said.

"Hell, I know he got the lynch bunch to kill Jack Perry . . . but what can I prove?" He answered that himself. "Not a damn' thing, Buck."

"Go ahead," Buck encouraged.

"Jack had to get lynched. He was throwing the dignity of the Hammerhead in the mud. Them Lawrences has been a proud clan. Curt is of the same bolt of cloth as was his father John. Jack murdered John Lawrence."

Buck asked, "Are you sure of that."

Potter kept on eating. "All the signs pointed towards Jack," he said.

Buck got to his boots and brushed off his levis. Tortilla Joe, with a heave, also got upright.

Clair watched.

Buck said, "Has Hammerhead lost cattle, Potter?"

The lawman nodded. "Curt Lawrence claims it has. He claims that the homesteaders are selling his cattle south in Sonora, across the Border. He says they're eatin' Hammerhead beef out at the dirt camp. I trailed cow sign, lost it. Never was no good with my nose to the ground."

"You're not sure, then?" Buck was persistent.

"Not sure. I might head into Phoenix town."

Buck asked, "Why?"

"Git the United States marshal's office to side me. Jail delivery is a serious offence, and if cattle are goin' across the line — thet makes it a federal offence. Might head out for Phoenix, I might."

Buck spoke slowly. "You say you left Buckskin because you was afraid somebody might kill you. Who was that *somebody*, Potter?"

The ox-like eyes rolled in moist sockets. "Do I have to say some names, McKee?"

"You'd sure help us clear this up," Buck answered.

The sheriff looked at Clair. He swung his moist gaze over to Tortilla Joe. The Mexican studied him in wicked intent. Potter did not like the look in the dark eyes. He looked back at Buckshot McKee.

"I won't say, McKee."

Buck nodded, seemingly satisfied. "All right, Potter." Suddenly, without warning, the flat of his hand went against the big chest, knocking Potter back. Potter grunted, the push turning him just enough so that Tortilla Joe's right fist, arching out of nowhere, socked the lawman hard under the jawbone.

Potter sank down like a pole-axed bull.

Tortilla Joe pushed the man flat with his boot. He jumped on the big belly with both boots, and his smile was wicked. Potter's breath whooshed out of him. He screamed, "You'll bust my big belly open!" and Tortilla Joe put a boot on the man's windpipe. Potter struggled, kicked, swatted, and then his face grew blue. It got as blue as a blue-roan horse. Then it went red. At this point, Tortilla Joe took his boot back. Potter sucked in air and then sat up and fear was wild across his bulging eyes.

"Don't kill — me — "

Potter stared up at Tortilla Joe. This time, for some reason, the Mexican did not have a long and stupid face. His face was rock-hard and rock-stern. Potter glanced at Clair, who watched fascinated; he swung his big eyes around to Buckshot McKee, who was grinning tightly.

"You gonna talk?" Buck asked.

"Well, now — " Potter shook his head. "Maybe no — "

Tortilla Joe said gleefully, "We streep all his clothes off, no. We let hees beeg belly get sunburned as he lay on the ant pile. Them red ants, they bite like a roadrunner — they have teensneeps for beaks. They make the belly crack open. Then the sun on that belly — Hola, he die slow, eh, Buckshots?"

Buck grinned. "Ant hill around back of this boulder. Seen it when we rode in. Black ants, though — some of them a half inch long, it looked like.

Will black ants be as good as red, Tortilla?"

"Better."

"Get him by the legs and drag him over to the pile. Hey, he don't want to play with us, eh?"

"I ain't got much to say," the sheriff said hurriedly. "So, I'll shoot off my mouth. I'm sure Halloway engineered that lynching, seeing Curt Lawrence was out chasin' this gal here. I was afraid either Lawrence or Halloway would try to kill me."

"Hell, Halloway is harmless, ain't he?" Buck asked. "Just a town banker, not a gunman."

"Him and Lawrence are good friends, remember that."

Buck smiled. Yeah, he thought, they're good friends — they're sharing the same wife. He asked, "Who owns the Hammerhead, sheriff?"

Potter had trouble with his throat. He had to clear his throat three times before he could answer.

"Lawrence owns it, of course.

Inherited it from old John."

"Any mor'gages on it?" Buck asked.

"I'm country recorder, Buck," the sheriff returned. "I'd know if there was a mor'gage, 'cause it would come for recording through my office. And there ain't none on record."

Buck mused with that bit of information. "Just had a wild idea that didn't work out, I reckon." He looked at Tortilla Joe. "Hades, Joe, this man is as dumb as we are."

"Dumber. Eet was a shame I had to jomp on his eentestines."

Potter glared at him. "I aim to jug you two some time for beatin' me up. After I come back with the marshal, I'll throw you two in my clink — an' toss the key in Salt River."

"You got any witnesses?" Buck asked.

"Witnesses to what?" the sheriff asked.

Buck shrugged. "You say we beat you up, Potter. Have you got anybody who seen us manhandle you?"

"Clair saw it."

Buck spoke to Clair. "You never seen nothin', honey. Hell, you couldn't testify against me, after spending a night in bed with me, could you?"

Potter's eyes bugged out like hen eggs. Tortilla Joe giggled like a schoolgirl who, for the first time, discovered she liked boys.

"He — slept with — you?" Potter's throat had recovered.

She did not blush. "I slept between him and Tortilla Joe in my room. We all had our clothes on. We slept on top of the covers. Don't get any bad ideas, Potter!"

Buck noticed that the seamstress had a very harsh voice. Underneath she was brassy and tough and domineering. He had detected these traits in her before, and he wondered if his first impression of her had not been wrong. When she had collided her horse with that of Tortilla Joe's, she had seemed girlish and naïve and womanly sweet. Now sometimes her language got harsh undertones and a tough fibre.

"You wouldn't want to help these two helions, would you, Clair?"

"I wouldn't help either of you."

The sheriff grinned. "Are you goin' to Phoenix with me, girl?"

"No!"

Potter rubbed his throat slowly. "My wife might tangle with you if you head back for Buckskin. The ol' lady is hell on high heels, Clair."

"I'm not afraid of the fat slob."

"Hell of a way to refer to a man's lovin' spouse," Potter grumbled. "The ol' lady won't go as far as to use a pistol or shotgun on you, Clair. But she sure can hit from the ground, thet ol' gal can. An' them long fingernails of hers — hell, you'll look like you matched claws with a wildcat, woman."

Clair spoke abruptly. "I'll chance that, sheriff."

Potter said, "Wish you'd stay with me, honey. We ran out of Buckskin together — you was congenial then. Hell, you even kissed me of your own free will, then. What changed your mind about me?"

"I got thinking of Buck," the girl joked, winking at one Buckshot McKee.

They mounted, leaving the sorrowful sheriff there in the rimrock. They rode down on the desert sand. Heat hit the sand, bounced, hit them, then rebounded to the sand. Buck said nothing. Tortilla Joe sang an old Mexican song softly, and his key was wild. Clair rode and said nothing.

They went to Cinchring camp.

Clair and Tortilla Joe went to the cook tent. Buck got Fiddlefoot Garner off to one side. They squatted in the shade of a giant saguaro cactus and talked. Buck did most of the talking.

The huge head of Fiddlefoot Garner mostly nodded affirmation. His head bobbed like a float on a fish-line when a carp is nibbling on the bait.

"This crew, Buck, has never et one bit of Hammerhead steak, unless it was bought from the butcher, down in town," Fiddlefoot Garner vowed. "We never stole a single Hammerhead cow."

"I'm not asking about a *single* cow," Buck pointed out, smiling. "I'm asking about more than one, Fiddlefoot."

"Quit your joshin', Buck. This is serious."

Buck climbed upward to his rawboned height. "Your word is tops with me, Garner."

Fiddlefoot Garner hammered one doubled fist into the palm of his hand. "If Lawrence is losin' cattle they're not goin' to this camp. If he keeps on pesterin' us farmers we'll stretch his hide out on a sandy spot in a dry wash and the hide will be full of bullet holes, believe you me!"

"Not so loud," Buck cautioned. "It's only five miles into Buckskin town. You'll knock over a house there with thet voice."

Fiddlefoot calmed down. "Where the hell did that stupid sheriff go?"

"I don't know," Buck said.

The trio left the camp, after Buck had eaten something. Fiddlefoot Garner watched them leave. He stood there in the blistering sun, coated with grimy sand, and he shook his head mournfully. He looked like a dehorned bull shaking his head to keep the blowflies away.

Buck glanced back.

"Big man," he said. "Got some brains, too."

"What did you two have that was so important to talk about?" Clair asked.

Buck said, "Women."

"Oh, joking all the time."

Buck said, "Would you like me more if I was the serious, studious type? You know — well dressed, good looking."

She looked at him. "You couldn't be that if you tried, McKee. All you are is a saddlebum . . ."

Buck smiled. "Keerect, honey. And that's what I aim to be the day I close my eyes for the last time. Sandpaper collars for roughnecks, you know."

"Your neck is too rough even for

rough sandpaper," she said, but she was smiling.

Buck spoke to Tortilla Joe. "You swing north, Tortilla, and scout the Hammerhead range there. Scout for signs of cattle on the move. Take Clair with you. She's safer with you than with me."

"Why?" Clair asked.

Buck looked at her. "I get you alone and I get bad ideas."

"I want to go with you."

Buck shook his head. "You're too much woman . . . I don't trust you or me, either. I ain't got my hammerlock hold down right yet, need more practice. I might get the worse of the tussle. Be ashamed as a man could be if a woman — a little woman like you — threw me . . . "

She stuck out her tongue at him.

"Right purty tongue," Buck complimented.

"Come on, Clair," Tortilla Joe said.

She and the Mexican headed north. Buck knew the general direction of the

Hammerhead ranch, and he rode that direction. Within thirty minutes he was on a sand ridge overlooking the ranch-house and buildings.

A big spread, he saw. Ironwood trees grew in the immense yard. He saw huge manzanita trees with red trunks shiny in the sun. He also saw the guard . . . before the guard had seen him.

He hollered, "Peaceful man coming in, guard!"

The man was squatting under the shade of an over-thrusting granite boulder. Buck's words jerked him to his feet. His rifle was half-raised when Buck rode in. Buck had his right hand high, palm out.

The guard watched him and didn't trust him. Buck saw a bowlegged man of about forty. The hammer on the Winchester .30-30 was at full cock. Buck had a cold spot in his belly.

"No trouble wanted," he said.

"You're McKee, ain't you?"

"I am."

"What do you want here on

Hammerhead?"

Buck said, "I want to talk to Curt Lawrence."

"He's in the house."

Buck asked, "His wife there, too?"

"Both in the house, I reckon."

Buck said, "Take me to them, friend."

The man's eyes narrowed. "Lawrence don't cotton to you, McKee. Get off on this side of your bronc. Watch your hands. Then walk ahead of me . . . an' remember this Winchester is ticklin' your long spine, *amigo*!"

Buck did as directed. They walked across the hoof-and boot-packed yard towards the rambling *hacienda*. Hammerhead men squatted in the shade of buildings and watched. Buck looked at them and marked them for what they were: gunmen. They said nothing, but they watched him.

Gun wolves.

The long porch was covered with native flagstone. Their boot heels made sounds across the porch. The guard knocked on a huge oaken door.

"The guard, Missus Lawrence."

"Come in," a woman's voice said.

The guard said, "Open the door and enter, McKee." The big door swung in silently and Buck was in a huge room. Flagstone was on the floor and over these slabs were gaudy Navajo and Chimayo blankets. A big fireplace made of native copper ore was at the far end. The furniture was made by hand and was made of manzanita. Hand-carved beams stretched across the open ceiling.

But Buck McKee was not interested in the house. His eyes were on the woman who sat in the big chair, her legs curled under her. Sybil Lawrence was crocheting; she looked demure and domestic. This rather surprised Buck. Always, to this time, she had appeared brassy hard and sophisticated.

"Take a chair, Mr. McKee," she said.

15

Range Talk

BUCK was a little surprised. He said, "I'll squat here," and he settled on his heels, back to the wall. He looked at the gunman. "You can go now, Junior. Your little day's work is through, child."

The gunman scowled, then looked at Sybil Lawrence.

Mrs. Lawrence said, "Thanks, John," and the gunman left. Buck heard his boots pound across the flagstone covered porch and then hit the gravel walk. Buck rolled a cigarette and asked, "Where is your old man?"

"In the library."

Buck had another surprise. It seemed odd to associate books with a person like Curt Lawrence. The interior of the room was cool. Sybil Lawrence kept on crocheting, her needle swift and sure. Buck watched her fingers. Sunlight came through a window and reflected facets of dancing light from her red hair.

Buck said, "Did you expect me?"

She didn't look up. "I thought maybe you'd come for a talk . . . sooner or later. Do you want to talk to Curt, too?"

"Will you call him?"

She called and Curt Lawrence answered. Buck heard him come down the hallway, boots making sounds. When he entered he scowled at Buck, who by this time had his smoke working.

"Okay, McKee. Talk fast and then get to hell out of here, savvy? What's on your mind, fella?"

Buck sucked his cigarette. "Don't jump into the collar too fast, big man. You're in trouble up to your bull-neck . . . and that neck of yours might get stretched for all you know . . . "

Curt Lawrence studied him. Sybil

Lawrence had stopped crocheting, her needlework lying in her lap.

"Did you ride out here to threaten me on my own property?" Curt Lawrence clipped his words.

Buck grinned. "Jes' stay cool . . . an' we'll settle somethin', Lawrence. Sheriff Henry Potter is headin' into Phoenix."

"What for?" Lawrence asked.

Buck got to his feet and crossed the room and threw his cigarette butt into the fireplace. Then he returned to his original position, back to the wall.

"He aims to get the United States Marshal into this," Buck said.

Curt Lawrence asked, "Where do I fit in, McKee?" His tone held derision.

"Jail delivery and a lynchin'," Buck said. "Two damned serious charges, Lawrence. Maybe charges so big that even the *Lawrence* name won't save your neck, eh?"

"Maybe I wasn't behind the lynchin'," Lawrence said.

Buck nodded. "Maybe you weren't,"

he agreed. "But this ranch has lost cattle . . . lots of cattle, hasn't it?"

Curt Lawrence looked at his wife. Sybil Lawrence's gaze met that of her husband. Then the woman looked at Buck McKee.

Sybil Lawrence said quietly, "Go on, Buck. I think you're barking up the right tree, Texan."

Buck said, "Yesterday me an' Tortilla Joe met you, Missus Lawrence, ridin' open range. Behin' you trailed your husban'. Evidently you were out scoutin' for your cattle. Maybe you don't know that, all the time, somebody was trailin' you."

"Who trailed us?" Lawrence's voice was husky.

Buck climbed to his boots. "I think you know, Lawrence." He put on his stetson. "Tortilla Joe an' me is ready to close this whole mess . . . for once and for always. We've got all the loose ends picked up, now . . ."

"I doubt that," Lawrence stated

Buck had his hand on the door-knob.

"Frankly, as far as I'm concerned, you can doubt and be damned, Lawrence. I came here to warn you, for the last time, to stay out of my way, savvy?"

"And if I don't stay out of your way?"

Buck said, "I'll kill you, Lawrence."

They looked at each other. Rage was in the eyes of the young cattle-king; Buck had no anger. He was merely stating a positive fact.

Lawrence said, huskily, "Why, you two bit drifter, I'll — "

But his wife cut in quickly. "Curt, watch your temper, please. Buck is speaking the truth, so please keep out of his way."

Curt Lawrence looked at his wife. Slowly the anger left him. "Sybil, I've stood about all I can hold, honey. I've been double-crossed from hell to Sunday. You're the only one, honey, who has stood by me."

"Buck's going to work this out, Curt. I know he is. Leave it to him." She spoke to Buck. "Thanks for calling, McKee."

"The pleasure," said Buck McKee, "is all mine, Missus Lawrence."

He left them, then. Left them in the coolness of the immense ranch-house built by old John Lawrence. His boots beat across the flagstone porch, and then found the gravel walk. As he crossed the compound the human wolves watched him. They had canine, ugly eyes. The guard had led his bronc into the shade of the huge rock barn.

Buck mounted and left the Hammerhead ranch.

He kept remembering Sybil Lawrence. She was fighting for her life, and she, being a woman, had only a woman's guiles, to fight with. But still, she was strong; her husband had obeyed her.

But what if it came to a showdown?

The shaggy wolf in Curt Lawrence, the fighting blood handed down from his fighting sire, would come through,

Buck knew. Buck realized, also, that this range was sitting on top of a hill filled with dynamite. Gunsmoke and gunflame might be the match needed to ignite the fuse . . .

He remembered the gunmen. Cold-eyed men of the saddle, hired for their gun slinging ability — not their riding prowess. This was costing Hammerhead a lot in way of dollars. Stolen steers and cows, and a bunch of gunmen on the payroll. That ran into lots of dollars, no matter from what angle the setup was viewed.

Buck left the creek and climbed a long alluvial cone, heading for the higher ridges. His plan was to gain altitude and pick out Tortilla Joe and Clair McCullen through his field glasses. Catsclaw snapped back, caught his shirt sleeve, and tore his sleeve, slightly touching his hide. "Wait-a-minute" some called this brush that, with its cats-claw branches, grabbed a man and tried to hold him. But Buck was not interested in the terrain. Nor was he interested in the brush that covered this wilderness here on the Salt River.

He was thinking of the Gallatin ranch, down where the Gila River and the Colorado joined forces, right outside of Yuma. He wanted to head south-west, and he wanted Tortilla Joe to ride with him. Down there they'd spend the winter punching cows, with maybe a few drinks occasionally in San Luis, the little town that hugged the International Border.

Old Man Gallatin would be glad to see them. Ma Gallatin would beam and welcome them in for chuck, and young Sonny, their grandson, would ride range with them — even if he had to sneak out of school to do it. Heck, Sonny would be thirteen now — or was it fourteen?

Buck searched the brush with his glasses. He saw cattle and he swept the glasses across the rangelands, endeavouring to pick out his partner and Clair McCullen.

This was an endless, tumbling range of desolation. Here lived the prairie wolf, the coyote, and occasionally one could hear the far-high scream of the travelling cougar. Mountains arose on the north, but the snow had left even their highest tips, the sun running across them and melting the snow. To the west stretched the desert — long and wide and grey with sand, its breast marked by green verde trees, by the green of mesquite.

To the east, the desert stretched also, but in the far distance it hit the mountains, and Buck could make out the blue lines of high peaks. He turned his direction towards the south. The desert moved on and on, stretching towards Old Mexico; occasionally rimrock ledges rose to break the floor of sand. These ridges were dark and black, miles away. Buck saw some cattle moving in a coulée. They ran as though they were afraid of something, and Buck moved his gaze up the gully.

He saw two riders.

Clair, and Tortilla Joe.

He turned his bronc and loped towards them. When he neared them he saw the rifle in Tortilla Joe's hands. Clair McCullen sat a still saddle, and then Tortilla Joe, recognition coming with certainty as Buck rode closer, shifted and lifted the Winchester, jamming it down securely into his saddle holster.

"Buck, what you find out?"

Buck told them.

Clair McCullen said, "These cattle . . . they're sure wild."

Tortilla Joe spat on a lizard. "Somebody he has been the ronnin' these cattles, Buck. They are afraid of the mans on the horsebacks. What we do now?"

Buck watched Clair McCullen.

"Tonight," he said, "the three of us rob a bank . . . "

Buck saw colour leave the woman's face. For a moment, her bottom lip trembled violently. Then she caught her emotions and became calm again. When she looked at Buck, he had discreetly turned his gaze over to Tortilla Joe.

"We rob a bank," he repeated.

16

Guns in the Night

THEY stood in the Mercantile, Buckskin's biggest store . . . which was not, after all, very big. Clair McCullen kept anxiously watching the front street through the big flyspecked window.

Buck joked. "Lookin' for a boy friend of yours, Clair?"

She shook her head. She was stone-serious. "I'm watching out for Sheriff Potter's wife, Buck. She might hear I'm in town and tie into me. She must be nuts, to think I couldn't get anything better than that fat sap of a husband of her's to run off with."

Buck said, "I'll fight your battles from here out, honey."

The skinny little storekeeper chimed in with, "Don't make no rash promises,

Mr. McKee. You wouldn't talk so big if you had ever met Mrs. Potter on the field of battle."

"You've tangled horns with her, eh?" Buck asked.

Tortilla Joe speared three crackers from the barrel. The storekeeper saw him, scowled, but said nothing. Tortilla Joe's shiny white teeth made noises on the crackers.

"One day she almost whupped me," the skinny man informed.

"What for?" Buck asked.

"Overcharged her a thin dime on her monthly bill. Now what can I do for you, sir?"

The partners and Clair had just ridden into Buckskin. They had created quite a sensation, especially because of Clair being with them, and gossip was buzzing — where was that fat sheriff named Henry Potter?

Kids peered in the window. Elders sauntered by the store, casually glancing inside. A few of the bolder women, thirsting for gossip, even entered the store. They made a pretence of looking at articles they apparently wanted to purchase. One old dame, complete to sun bonnet, stood at a counter a few feet away, looking at some yard-goods, running the gingham through her fingers, her head cocked to hear any possible conversation.

"She get her earful of cuss words eef she leesens too close," Tortilla Joe said, grinning widely.

The woman glanced at him. Her face reddened and she walked away without a word, her back poker-straight.

The merchant repeated, "What will it be, sir?"

Buck asked, "Have you got any black blastin' powder?"

The skinny man's big eyes studied him. "Yes, I have some, sir. I suppose you are taking it out to the dam site for blasting purposes, huh?"

"That's it," Buck lied.

The man had the powder in a cellar on the edge of town. Buck ordered very little. The merchant said it was hardly worth the trouble of going out to the store-room to get such a small amount. Buck said, "I need other stuff, too," so this pleased the man, who sent his assistant to the powder-house, warning him not to smoke in the cellar.

The boy said, "Do I look that nutty, pop?"

The boy left. The storekeeper sighed. "Oh, for the chance to be a boy again, and to know more than my parents . . . " He squinted over his specs at Buck. "What else does you crave, cowboy?"

Clair McCullen kept watching the window. She seemed very nervous, Buck noticed. Discreetly the tall Texan grinned.

Tortilla Joe swiped two crackers from the barrel.

"I want some steel drills," Buck said.

He bought four drills — all in the three-quarter inch size. By now the merchant was scowling in puzzlement. What would a cowpuncher do with steel drills? He was bursting with curiosity that lack of familiarity required he did not voice.

"Anything else, sir?"

"One fuse," Buck said.

"That's in the powder-house. I'll send my other son to get it."

Buck nodded.

Tortilla Joe munched crackers. Clair watched the window. Buck asked. "Have you got a breast drill?"

"No, but I have a carpenter's brace," the merchant said.

Buck had no other choice than to buy the brace. He inserted a drill into it and tightened it down. A man who had just entered watched him. Buck shot this man a quick glance.

"Howdy, Banker Halloway," he said jovially.

Tortilla Joe smiled widely, cracker crumbs on his bottom lip. "Well, the banker," he said in greeting. "How are you todays, señor?"

From the tone of voices the two partners used one would never imagine

Buck had once knocked the banker down. They seemed happy and good-natured, as though the past were dead . . . forever. Some of this infectious feeling must have gripped the banker.

"Howdy, men."

"Nice days," Tortilla Joe chimed.

Buck noticed that Halloway sent a sharp glance towards Clair McCullen. The seamstress merely nodded her head; she did not speak. Halloway looked down at Buck's purchases. He seemed agreeable and forgiving.

"Going to do some blasting at the dam, Mr. McKee?"

"I am."

Halloway picked up a drill. He turned it between thumb and forefinger. Buck noticed the man's nails were clean, his hands had no callouses.

"Sort of a small hole to put powder in, eh?" the banker asked.

"We'll pour it in," Buck said.

"Oh." The lips formed the word almost silently.

Tortilla Joe spoke around a mouthful

of crackers. "We had better get the wreckin' bar, too, Buckshots. An' we need more .45 bullets for our gons, no?"

"That's right," Buck agreed.

Scowling, the merchant got a wrecking bar, laid it on the counter. Halloway scowled as he watched Buck inspect the bar. Finally Buck announced the bar as passing his inspection.

"How much for the mess?" Buck asked.

The boys had arrived with the fuse and the powder. The merchant did some figuring on a piece of wrapping paper. One of the boys waited on Banker Halloway, who wanted some cigarette papers. Buck paid the merchant and he and Tortilla Joe and the seamstress left, going to their horses at the livery barn. The hostler was out. Buck saw to it that their broncs had lots of hay. He gave them all a measure of oats in the feed-boxes, too.

"We'll need fresh, fast horses for our

get-away," he told Clair.

The woman spoke in an uncertain tone. "You mean, Buck — we still will rob Halloway's bank?"

"We sure do," Buck returned.

"But . . . for why?"

Buck studied her. "Why does anybody rob a bank?" he demanded.

"Well . . . for the money, of course."

Buck winked at Tortilla Joe. Clair did not see the wink. "There's lots of dinero in that bank. Lawrence keeps his dough there. We get the whole caboodle and turn the money over to Fiddlefoot Garner. Then him an' his farmers can build their dam and canals. And they can build them on Lawrence money . . . "

Tortilla Joe grinned. "We no keep the dinero, savvy? We geeve eet away. We be like the Robin Hood, no?"

She asked, slowly, "Have you boys ever robbed a bank before?"

Again, that wink, unseen by Clair. "We sure have," Buck said seriously. He gave her a hard and long look.

"Why are you — staring at me?" she asked.

Buck grabbed her thin shoulders. He shook her violently. She gasped, tried to break his grip, and failed.

"What's the matter with you, McKee?" she panted.

Buck spoke in a harsh tone. "You're gettin' cold boots. If you ever think of squealin' on us, sister, we'll cut out your purty gizzard, savvy. You're going out of this town with us. And you're going to keep your mouth shut all the time, understand?"

"Buck — You hurt me — "

Buck gripped her savagely. "You heard me, sister! You even think of squealing, and you'll not live long . . . even if you have got a purty face and a nice body. You won't get away from us now. You know too much, young lady."

"That ees righto," Tortilla Joe chimed in.

Slowly she got Buck's fingers loose. "I heard you, Buckshot. Yes, I'm with you, boys . . . to the bitter end, or however the end turns out. They lynched the only man I ever loved. I'm sick and tired of this stupid town and its stupid, prying people. You can count on me, gentlemen."

"Now she ees call us gentlemans," Tortilla Joe said. "First time she meet us, she call us cuss names."

"I didn't know you then like I do now," Clair McCullen said.

Buck said, "Come dark we'll lead our horses up the alley behind the bank. Get them ready for a fast get-away out of this burg. Like we did when we sprung that bank up in Wyomin', Tortilla Joe. We got to get some chuck packed and some blankets, too. We got blankets for us but we need some for Clair. You got a long, hard ride ahead of you, honey. We head south into Old Mexico. Loaf around there for six months or so until things quieten, and we'll live like two kings and a queen."

"Then what?" she asked.

Buck was getting warmed up; his

imagination was running on fast hoofs. "We slip north acrost the Border and stick up another bank. Over in Texas, maybe. Then we drift into Old Mexico again."

"Good," she said.

Buck said, "Now we go to your place, Clair. Spend the day there — what is left of it — loafing and getting ready for tonight. Too bad that damn' banker came in when I was buyin' that black powder and that fuse."

"He hasn't got brains enough to be suspicious," she said. "He's too dumb to count marbles."

"Bet he can count the dineros though," Tortilla Joe said.

"All bankers kin do that," Buck said.

They went to Clair's house. Tortilla Joe promptly kicked off his boots and flopped on the bunk. Clair busied herself getting some clothes packed and ready for the get-away trip. She would take just an extra pair of levis and a shirt. Buck said they would have to travel light. An extra pound on a bronc might slow him down to the point where a posse could catch him.

He put it on thick and scary. He noticed, at times, that her eyes would grow small and scheming, but those were the times when she thought nobody was watching her.

When they looked at her, she was always smiling. But the smile, Buck noticed, was forced. He had been all wrong in judging these two women. He remembered watching pretty Sybil Lawrence standing on tiptoe and kissing Halloway, there in the bank.

She had been playing a game — and she had been playing it because she loved her husband, Curt Lawrence. Sybil, Buck thought, was a good actress, one of the best he had ever seen. He compared her with Clair McCullen. Mrs. Lawrence stood out head and shoulders above the seamstress. Buck shrugged it off, blaming it on fickle fate. He was a little jittery inside. He hoped his plan would work. It had to work.

He and Tortilla Joe had to leave this town. Tomorrow would be the inquest, for the coroner had come over from the neighbouring county; Sheriff Potter was gone, he could not sit as coroner. Rumour had it that the body of Jack Perry would go into the fill of the dam, and the dam would be his grave. A fitting memorial, Buck thought. Jack, whom he had never seen, would lie forever in the dam he had constructed, had planned, had died for.

Buck said, "I have to get some Bull Durham and papers."

Clair said, "Be careful, Buck. This town has Lawrence gunmen in it."

Buck said, "I'll be careful, child."

He went to the saloon. Thick Neck looked at him, sold him Durham and wheat straw papers, looked like he was full of advice, but Buck did not give him a chance to talk.

"Nice day," Buck said.

"Good day," Thick Neck said.

Buck walked towards the bank. The eyes of Buckskin town were on him.

Clair did not know that he had ridden over to the Hammerhead and had talked with Curt Lawrence and his wife. He had reported his conversation back to Tortilla Joe, but that had been on the side — Clair had not heard them talk.

Buck felt the desert heat hit him. He felt, also, a sort of relief, for this would soon be over. Neither he nor Tortilla Joe had as yet written to old Sam Perry about his son's untimely death. Later they would write, but by then this would be solved.

Or maybe they would not write. Maybe they would be both dead . . .

Buck smiled tightly. This was an odd deal. Here they were battling for a man they had never met, and that man was dead — a lynch mob had hanged him. But an old man — a good old man — a sick old man — was up in Colorado, and the hanged man had been the old man's son . . .

Buck turned into the bank.

Halloway looked up from his desk.

263

"Hello, McKee," he said. "Some favour I can do for you?"

Buck dug in his pant's pocket. He came out with a gold piece. "My last twenty bucks," he said with a grin. "A man's summer wages goes hell a-kitin' fast, eh?"

"That they do."

Buck said, "I'm driftin' out come daylight. Some of these small places ain't got change for a twenty, so guess I'll change it here — if you'll give me some silver for it. Damned sorry I hit you, Mister Halloway."

The banker smiled and rubbed his jaw. "Still a mite sore." He got patronizing and genial. "Maybe I asked for it, McKee."

He opened a cash drawer and got some change. Buck and he talked for a while. Both seemed congenial enough; still, inside of each, despite their friendly talk, was a guarded stiffness.

Buck got the impression that this sleek banker was feeling him out.

Halloway was jabbing here, probing at this point. Buck had a definite purpose for talking to the banker, and for entering the bank. It had not been because he wanted a twenty dollar gold piece cashed, either.

He said. "So long, sir, and continued good luck."

"Glad to have met you, McKee."

Buck walked down the main street. He met Clair and said, "Thought you'd stay close to the home wigwam. Figured you was afraid of Mrs. Potter."

"She's home sick with *la grippe*," the girl said. "Even if she wasn't sick, I'd walk the street with complete indifference. I'm a citizen and a taxpayer."

"I've said that a few times, too," Buck reminded. "Didn't keep me from gettin' beat up, honey. Take care of yourself."

"Where have you been?" she wanted to know.

Buck said, "First, to the saloon for tobacco. Then, I cased the bank

— cashed a twenty-buck gold piece as a blind to get inside and look around."

"Will it be easy to — crack?"

"Like openin' a tin of bakin' soda," Buck said. "All we need is a can opener and a screwdriver . . . and some black powder for the safe."

"Oh . . . "

Buck said, "Where are you going?"

She said she was going to the store. Buck said he was going back to her room. They left. She crossed the street to the Mercantile. Buck went between two buildings and came out on the alley. The thought came that this alley had seen a lot of excitement the last few days. Will March had died in the alley, blood soaking into Arizona sand. He remembered Sitting Bull Jones knocking out Hawkins. The gunman had come to, and he had been sitting in a garbage barrel in this alley. Buck had heard that Lawrence had run Hawkins off this range.

Buck watched, saw what he wanted, and then went to Clair McCullen's house. Tortilla Joe sat on the bed and chewed a tortilla in noisy contentment. He rolled big brown eyes and looked at Buck.

"What you find out, *amigo*?"

Buck sat on a chair. He shoved his long legs out and seemed interested in his unpolished and scuffed boots. He remembered the fine polished boots of Banker Halloway. The difference between the man who worked and the man who did not work was a quarter, he had heard somebody say.

And the gink who did not work was the one who had the twenty-five cent piece, so the joke had run.

"How we rob thees bank, Buckshots?"

Buck said, "The bank roof has a skylight. I'll get in the back door. You stay up on the roof and watch through the skylight. I'll be the pig in a poke. The piece of human meat in the trap. The bait for the whole thing."

"Eef theese work right, I come down through the skylight, no. Weeth my pistola out, eh?"

"That's it, Tortilla Joe."

The Mexican felt of his teeth. "I steel got them all," he said after a while. "I bite into a rock in thees tortilla. How far ees eet from the roof to the floor?"

"Eight feet ceiling."

"Long way for a fat man to drop," the Mexican said.

"I'll bring some pillows," Buck said sarcastically. "Put them on the floor to break your fall."

He told about meeting Clair McCullen. Tortilla Joe nodded.

Within a few minutes, Clair entered. Tortilla Joe chewed on what seemed an endless chain of tortillas. His jaws crackled on them like the jaws of an Ohio hog eating corn. Clair sat on the bed beside Buck. Dust came and turned into night; they sat there in silence. The night held its sounds of dogs and burros and people, and then these fell asleep. Clair now dozed and Tortilla Joe dozed beside her, but Buck McKee did not sleep.

He had moved over to the rocking-chair. Despite his raw nerves, he sat with his legs out in front of him. The room became pitch dark.

Tortilla Joe started to snore.

Buck waited another hour or so. Then he lit a match and looked at his watch. He said, "It's that time, folks."

Tortilla Joe came awake. "Time to rob a bank, no?"

"Yes," Buck said.

17

Gun Trap

BUCK picked up the crowbar. He got the powder in a sack, saw that the fuse was in the bag, also. Then he put a drill into the brace.

He gave last minute instructions.

"Tortilla Joe, you go across the street. Stand in the shadows in front of Thick Neck's saloon."

"*Si*, Buckshots."

"Watch the door of the bank. The front door."

"*Si, amigo*."

Clair asked, "What's my job?"

"You watch the back door. I jimmy it and go inside. You cover my back, and Tortilla Joe covers my front."

Her voice was a little unsteady. "You think you can crack the safe,

Buck? It's a big safe."

Buck's voice oozed a confidence he did not feel. "I've cracked them afore . . . an' I'll crack them again. The bigger they are the easier they are to bust into. Thet safe looks like a tin can. A little hole an' some powder an' the fuse and then a little bit of a *boom*. And the door'll pop open as fast as the eyes of an ol' maid comin' upon some kids in a swimmin' hole plumb naked!"

There was a moment pause. Outside Buckskin town slept. There was a sliver of a moon, but it had little light as yet. The lamp sputtered and spat. Buck looked at Clair. Her thin face was set, her lips tight. Tortilla Joe's wide and dark face was an emotionless expanse of human flesh.

"We all know our jobs?" Buck asked.

"I do, Buckshots."

Clair said, "Let's go . . . "

They slipped out into the night. Buck carried the safecracking equipment. Within the tall cowpuncher was the fervent hope that this would work out all right. He was taking a big chance. He was making himself a human guineapig in this experiment.

They went down the alley, Buck in the lead. The girl followed and behind stumbled fat Tortilla Joe. He seemed to fall over every can on the strip. Buckskin was silent and Buckskin was asleep. Buckskin was seemingly lazy and tired and under the dark cloak of slumber. But it seemed to Buck McKee that, under this cloak of indifference, lurked a great and subtle danger.

They came to the rear door of the bank. Black and ugly, the building reared against the moon, which had gathered strength quickly.

Tortilla Joe whispered hoarsely. "I leave you two at thees point, an' I go across the street, no?"

"Okay," Buck said.

"I watch the front of the bank," the Mexican said.

He lumbered into the night, dark and heavy. Buck and Clair stood and looked at the rear door of the bank.

"What are we waiting for?" She shivered as she whispered her question.

"Wait till Tortilla Joe gets stationed," he said quietly.

He counted to fifty, then he stationed her in the alley. The dark shadows hid her. He went to the back door. With a hard, vicious jab, he drove the sharp end of the wrecking bar down, smashing it between the edge of the door and the jamb. It made a dull sound against the dried wood.

He drove it in further.

Again, the sharp end cut pine wood. He laid his weight against the bar, but the door held.

Again, he jabbed the crowbar into the slot. Again, he laid his weight against it.

The wood creaked. The door gave in slightly, then the lock held. Buck put everything he had against the crowbar. The steel bent. The latch left the lock.

The door silently swung in.

Buck dropped the crowbar to the sand. It fell with a soft sound. He thought, Here it is, and he went inside the dark bank. He closed the door behind him. But, because of the broken lock, the door would not latch shut.

For a moment, he hunkered there, dark against the wall. He listened. He heard the dull slide of something across the roof. To the average ears, it would sound like maybe a bird had a nest on the roof, and was stirring around.

Buck thought, Good old Tortilla Joe.

He had spotted a long window-stick in the corner. He got this and he opened the skylight, finding the catch and pushing upward. A hand came down, found the end of the window-stick, and released it from the prong.

"I am ready, Buckshots," the voice came, from the roof.

Buck lit a lamp. He left it turned low. He turned his attention to the safe. Strangely, he was remembering old Sam Perry's whiskery, pain-filled face. Sam had had but one joy in life — and now that joy, that pride, was dead. Hanged by lynchers from the jutting beam of the court-house . . .

Buck had never opened a safe before. He did not know where to begin. Logic told him to act like he was going to drill a hole. He put his tools on the floor. He looked at the bit in the brace.

He had expected the man to come in from the alley.

Instead, the man came from a side room. He came silently and he came in behind Buck, who had one eye on the door.

The man held a .45 revolver. His face was grim, and his voice was a tough snarl as he said, "Turn around, McKee. And with your hands up high, too."

Buck had placed his own .45 on a nearby chair. He turned and his belly had a tight knot in it. Wouldn't anything work out right? He wondered if the man had heard him open the skylight and had heard Tortilla Joe's hissed words from the roof?

The man had silently opened a door leading to another room. The thought came to Buck that, when the door had been closed, the sounds made by Tortilla Joe had not entered the room, and therefore this man did not know the Mexican was on the roof, poised over the open skylight.

That was an element in his favour.

But there was one thing definitely not in his favour. He had hoped to get the drop on this man first; instead, the fellow had his .45 on him. And it was level and tough-looking, with the lamplight glowing on it.

Buck spoke clearly so Tortilla Joe would be able to hear. "Halloway, eh?" he said.

"The end of your trail, McKee!"

"Well," Buck asked. "What have you got to say in your defence, banker?"

The banker's eyes widened with surprise. "What have *I* got to say?" Surprise blunted the hard edge of his voice. "You're the gent that should have something to say . . . and say it damned fast. You're robbin' my bank. A serious offence, McKee, and one for which you'll get killed."

Halloway cocked the .45.

The click was a loud sound. He looked big and tough, standing there with the big .45. Buck glanced at his own Colt. It was only five feet away, but it looked like it was a half-mile in the distance. The thought came that he might get killed here in the bank.

And that thought was not pleasant.

Buck spoke as clearly as he could. "You and the woman played it close, Halloway. She played up to Jack Perry. Fiddlefoot Garner's conversation with me put me wise."

Halloway asked, "Wise to what, McKee?"

Buck was stalling for time. Tortilla Joe should drop through the skylight any moment now.

"She pumped Perry for inside information about the dam. She then turned this over to you. Then Sybil Lawrence played up to you. You hold notes on Hammerhead. The Lawrences told me that today."

"You talk smart, McKee."

Buck watched the .45. He would go out fighting, he decided. Why didn't Tortilla Joe drop down through that skylight? Surely the Mexican could see . . . and hear . . . Buck again glanced at his own .45.

"Go on," Martin Halloway ordered.

"You didn't record the notes. That left Potter in the lurch. He never knew Hammerhead owed you money. So Sybil played up to you — tried to get inside dope — but you were too slick. You already had one woman."

"Did that damned woman talk — did she tell you this.?"

Buck said, "I got a promise from the Lawrences that might interest you, Halloway. They said that if I cleared this up, they'd not bother Cinchring any more."

Halloway's tongue darted out. He

wet his thin lips. His eyes were on Buck — beady, scheming eyes.

"Go on, McKee. I'm curious."

"You and Clair McCullen came into Buckskin at the same time. You two saw your chance to hit something big. You both wanted Hammerhead. So . . . you've had a gang stealin' Hammerhead cattle. You tried to break the ranch from that angle. You laid the blame on young Perry's construction workers."

"That's right, McKee."

The back door opened. Clair McCullen silently entered. Halloway glanced at her.

"Did you talk, woman?"

"Not a word, Martin."

She had a gun and her eyes were steel-hard. They glistened in the lamplight. She was not soft and feminine now. She was a female killer with her lips peeled back and her gun in her hand.

Buck said, "Clair, you killed old John Lawrence. Shot him down on open range, and laid the blame on Perry. You bawled when you mentioned Perry's name to me. You loved him, you said — you loved him enough to lead him to a hangman's noose."

"What do you mean?" she demanded hoarsely.

Buck said, "You deliberately led that Lawrence posse out of town so your lover here could get a mob and lynch Perry. Lawrence really didn't want a lynchin', but you engineered it . . . knowing the blame would be laid on Lawrence. You worked Cinchring against Hammerhead."

Her eyes glowed. "Buck, I never killed old John. Halloway shot him — from behind — from the brush . . . "

Halloway snarled, "Close your mouth, woman!"

But Clair kept on talking. And her gun was rigid. She spoke out of the corner of her mouth and she put the words up to Halloway.

"I'm going to get rid of you. You got your will made out leaving everything you own to me. Now is my chance to get rid of you. If McKee goes down — then I shoot at you — If you go down, then I kill McKee. And when it is over, I'll kill the Mexican, and everybody will be silenced. And I'll own this and the notes on Hammerhead."

Buck gave her plan quick thought. She was right . . . if Halloway's will were made out to her.

"You'll never get Tortilla Joe," he said.

She said, "I'll just walk up to him . . . across the street . . . and I'll kill him. Or when he runs in here I'll waylay him. Two would be bank robbers . . . and a dead banker."

She stood directly under the skylight. Suddenly the Mexican fell down. He came down hard and he hit her on the head and shoulders.

Buck heard her surprised gasp.

Then, the tall Texan was going for his gun. He hit the chair and snagged the .45 and he rolled over, crashing against the wall. One glance showed him that

281

Tortilla Joe was on the floor. Clair McCullen was on her feet, though.

And she was shooting.

Halloway shot at Buck, and he missed because Buck was rolling. He screamed, "I got you, McKee!" and he swung his gun on Tortilla Joe. Just then Clair McCullen shot the banker in the chest.

Tortilla Joe had rolled to the far wall. He sat there with his .45 out. Buck shot him a glance and said, "He got confused. He missed me, *amigo*."

Tortilla Joe did not shoot.

Buck did not shoot, either.

There was no need of their firing their pistols. This had simmered down to a battle between a banker and an unscrupulous woman. Halloway and Clair McCullen had eyes only for each other. Buck watched in horrified fascination. Back to the wall, Tortilla Joe stared, lamplight on his level .45.

He saw a quivering go over Halloway's big body. He went to his knees, bending at the waist; Buck saw blood on the white silk shirt. But, as he went down, he fired twice.

His first bullet hit Clair McCullen. The second missed, but the first did the job.

Halloway looked at her, lying there on the floor. He dropped his gun and his fingers drew in and made his hands hard fists.

He looked at Tortilla Joe. "Come in through the skylight, eh? Thought I heard a sound up there — but pack rats . . . they run across the roof . . . " He looked at Buck. "She warned me today . . . of your plan. I aimed to pull a doublecross on her, but she beat me to it . . . "

Buck watched, throat dry.

Tortilla Joe lowered his gun.

Halloway's dark eyes touched the Mexican. They swung over to Buck McKee. Blood was coming down the white shirt, soaking into it. Buck had a moment of sorrow for this man who plainly was dead on his knees.

"We've been married seven years,"

the banker said slowly. "We worked this game — and it went sour on us. They want us both back east — bank embezzlement — They can come after us . . . now."

Halloway looked at the dead woman. Buck saw a tender feeling come over his face. He heard the slow, hesitant words.

"I'm sorry, sweetheart, I killed you . . . But wait just a minute, and I'll be with you, Clair . . . "

Halloway lay on the floor, then. He put his head on his arm and Buck could see his eyes.

The eyes went blank.

Buck got to his boots, knees shaky. "Never got to fire a shot," he murmured. He got Clair's wrist. Warm, but no blood pulsing through it. He looked at Halloway's body.

"You know the secret now, Halloway," the Texan drawled. "But you won't come back . . . to tell about it."

Tortilla Joe crossed himself.

They went down the alley towards the

livery-barn. Buckskin had come awake. People were going towards the bank. Some were pulling on their clothes as they hurried.

Somewhere a dog howled.

Suddenly Buck remembered the body of young Jack Perry, swinging slowly in the wind. Then, a dog had howled, too.

Maybe it was the same dog that now howled.

They rode out of town. "We settled a whale of a lot in a few days," Buck said. "In one way, they got their just desserts — they ambushed John Lawrence, hung Jack Perry."

Tortilla Joe nodded. "Where we go now?"

"We ride to the Lawrence ranch. Lawrence sent that gunman, Will March, against me, remember? I aim to work the big son over a little with my six-shooter barrel, if I get a chance."

"Then where we go, Buckshots?"

"We head for the Gallatin spread. We gotta write that letter to ol' Sam

Perry, too. But now we can tell him his son sleeps in peace, Tortilla Joe.

The Mexican nodded. "Jack he sleeps in peace," he said solemnly.

THE END

FIGHTING RAMROD
Charles N. Heckelmann

Most men would have cut their losses, but Frazer counted the bullets in his guns and said he'd soak the range in blood before he'd give up another inch of what was his.

LONE GUN
Eric Allen

Smoke Blackbird had been away too long. The Lequires had seized the Blackbird farm, forcing the Indians and settlers off, and no one seemed willing to fight! He had to fight alone.

THE THIRD RIDER
Barry Cord

Mel Rawlins wasn't going to let anything stand in his way. His father was murdered, his two brothers gone. Now Mel rode for vengeance.

ARIZONA DRIFTERS
W. C. Tuttle

When drifting Dutton and Lonnie Steelman decide to become partners they find that they have a common enemy in the formidable Thurston brothers.

TOMBSTONE
Matt Braun

Wells Fargo paid Luke Starbuck to outgun the silver-thieving stagecoach gang at Tombstone. Before long Luke can see the only thing bearing fruit in this eldorado will be the gallows tree.

HIGH BORDER RIDERS
Lee Floren

Buckshot McKee and Tortilla Joe cut the trail of a border tough who was running Mexican beef into Texas. They stopped the smuggler in his tracks.

BRETT RANDALL, GAMBLER
E. B. Mann

Larry Day had the choice of running away from the law or of assuming a dead man's place. No matter what he decided he was bound to end up dead.

THE GUNSHARP
William R. Cox

The Eggerleys weren't very smart. They trained their sights on Will Carney and Arizona's biggest blood bath began.

THE DEPUTY OF SAN RIANO
Lawrence A. Keating and
Al. P. Nelson

When a man fell dead from his horse, Ed Grant was spotted riding away from the scene. The deputy sheriff rode out after him and came up against everything from gunfire to dynamite.

FARGO: MASSACRE RIVER
John Benteen

The ambushers up ahead had now blocked the road. Fargo's convoy was a jumble, a perfect target for the insurgents' weapons!

SUNDANCE: DEATH IN THE LAVA
John Benteen

The Modoc's captured the wagon train and its cargo of gold. But now the halfbreed they called Sundance was going after it . . .

HARSH RECKONING
Phil Ketchum

Five years of keeping himself alive in a brutal prison had made Brand tough and careless about who he gunned down . . .

FARGO: PANAMA GOLD
John Benteen

With foreign money behind him, Buckner was going to destroy the Panama Canal before it could be completed. Fargo's job was to stop Buckner.

FARGO:
THE SHARPSHOOTERS
John Benteen

The Canfield clan, thirty strong were raising hell in Texas. Fargo was tough enough to hold his own against the whole clan.

PISTOL LAW
Paul Evan Lehman

Lance Jones came back to Mustang for just one thing — revenge! Revenge on the people who had him thrown in jail.

HELL RIDERS
Steve Mensing

Wade Walker's kid brother, Duane, was locked up in the Silver City jail facing a rope at dawn. Wade was a ruthless outlaw, but he was smart, and he had vowed to have his brother out of jail before morning!

DESERT OF THE DAMNED
Nelson Nye

The law was after him for the murder of a marshal — a murder he didn't commit. Breen was after him for revenge — and Breen wouldn't stop at anything . . . blackmail, a frameup . . . or murder.

DAY OF THE COMANCHEROS
Steven C. Lawrence

Their very name struck terror into men's hearts — the Comancheros, a savage army of cutthroats who swept across Texas, leaving behind a bloodstained trail of robbery and murder.

SUNDANCE: SILENT ENEMY
John Benteen

A lone crazed Cheyenne was on a personal war path. They needed to pit one man against one crazed Indian. That man was Sundance.

LASSITER
Jack Slade

Lassiter wasn't the kind of man to listen to reason. Cross him once and he'll hold a grudge for years to come — if he let you live that long.

LAST STAGE TO GOMORRAH
Barry Cord

Jeff Carter, tough ex-riverboat gambler, now had himself a horse ranch that kept him free from gunfights and card games. Until Sturvesant of Wells Fargo showed up.

McALLISTER ON THE COMANCHE CROSSING
Matt Chisholm

The Comanche, McAllister owes them a life — and the trail is soaked with the blood of the men who had tried to outrun them before.

QUICK-TRIGGER COUNTRY
Clem Colt

Turkey Red hooked up with Curly Bill Graham's outlaw crew. But wholesale murder was out of Turk's line, so when range war flared he bucked the whole border gang alone . . .

CAMPAIGNING
Jim Miller

Ambushed on the Santa Fe trail, Sean Callahan is saved by two Indian strangers. But there'll be more lead and arrows flying before the band join Kit Carson against the Comanches.

GUNSLINGER'S RANGE
Jackson Cole

Three escaped convicts are out for revenge. They won't rest until they put a bullet through the head of the dirty snake who locked them behind bars.

RUSTLER'S TRAIL
Lee Floren

Jim Carlin knew he would have to stand up and fight because he had staked his claim right in the middle of Big Ike Outland's best grass.

THE TRUTH ABOUT
SNAKE RIDGE
Marshall Grover

The troubleshooters came to San Cristobal to help the needy. For Larry and Stretch the turmoil began with a brawl and then an ambush.

WOLF DOG RANGE
Lee Floren

Will Ardery would stop at nothing, unless something stopped him first — like a bullet from Pete Manly's gun.

DEVIL'S DINERO
Marshall Grover

Plagued by remorse, a rich old reprobate hired the Texas Trouble-shooters to deliver a fortune in greenbacks to each of his victims.

GUNS OF FURY
Ernest Haycox

Dane Starr, alias Dan Smith, wanted to close the door on his past and hang up his guns, but people wouldn't let him.

DONOVAN
Elmer Kelton

Donovan was supposed to be dead. Uncle Joe Vickers had fired off both barrels of a shotgun into the vicious outlaw's face as he was escaping from jail. Now Uncle Joe had been shot — in just the same way.

CODE OF THE GUN
Gordon D. Shirreffs

MacLean came riding home, with saddle tramp written all over him, but sewn in his shirt-lining was an Arizona Ranger's star.

GAMBLER'S GUN LUCK
Brett Austen

Gamblers seldom live long. Parker was a hell of a gambler. It was his life — or his death . . .